ESCAPING OBSCURITY

Evergreen Series II

JOANN HERLEY

ACKNOWLEDGEMENTS

Cover Illustration by: © Summerlily | Dreamstime.com
Formatted by: P. Maier

DEDICATION

To my husband, Gene, I love you always and forever.

To my children, Brian and Holly, for giving me a million wonderful memories. I look forward to the next million.

SPECIAL THANKS

To Pam for helping with the little stumbling blocks of this book. You selected Gautier to be Kayleigh's warlock. You were willing to read each and every rough chapter as it left my fingertips. You kept Velsa's spell under control, thank heavens! Even after reviewing a dozen options, you helped me choose the perfect cover.

To my Lunch Team (John, Pam, Rachel, Dina, Dustin, and sometimes Sue) for listening, encouraging, and never laughing.

To Julie and Tailyr, for taking time out of your busy schedule to read my manuscripts.

HISTORY OF THE ISLAND OF ALLTREE

Long ago, strong ships carrying brave explorers discovered its lush forests, fertile earth and crystal clear rivers. Hearing of the beauty of the land, Lord Evergreen boarded a ship and sailed to Alltree to see the land for himself. Captured by its beauty, he returned home to tell everyone of the faraway island and his plans to build Evergreen Castle. Returning to Alltree with skilled craftsmen, he proceeded to build a castle on the west side of the island that overlooked the sea. After a decade, his castle was finally complete, and he brought his family to the island.

One by one, Lords Cumberland, Fallon, Draglaw, and Heinrich made their journey to Alltree and began building castles of their own. They were all peace loving men, and the five lords pledged to refrain from war and live in peace.

It wasn't long before immortals heard of the island and began to sneak aboard ships to make their way to Alltree. Once they arrived, they changed everything.

Prologue

Lara could see the brilliant stars filling the evening sky over Evergreen Castle while she lingered among the soft bed linens. Resting against the large feather pillows, she thought about her past and what the future might hold for herself and Thomas. She had found Thomas, quite by accident, and saved him from the madness of blood lust. In return, when she had desperately needed him, he had willingly bargained his sight to save her and brought her safely back home to Evergreen. He was brave and strong, as well as, the most tender lover. He was hers for all eternity, and she looked forward to spending every day wrapped in his arms. She was the happiest she had ever been in over two hundred years.

Knowing Thomas had left their bed before sunset; Lara sat up and moved her legs out from under the bed linens. She stood sliding her feet into the satin slippers left by her bed. Retrieving her long tunic, she pulled it over her head covering her naked body and walked over to the fire that Thomas had kindly fed before his leaving. She watched the flames dance among the logs mesmerized by the variety of its bright colors of orange, gold and vivid red. Memories of her sister, Magna, came to mind as she focused on the red of the flames.

How different we are from one another, she thought, as a bit of sadness made her eyes start to water.

Lara had tried for decades to help her younger sister, but Magna had willingly let the madness control her, becoming too evil and far beyond saving. Since ordering Magna's arrest for torturing and drinking the blood of humans, Lara feared her sister would not hesitate to deliver a final death to her if they should ever meet.

As she moved toward the window, she pushed Magna from her thoughts. Lara smiled, as she let the memories of Thomas' passionate kisses fill her mind. She stood at the window and gazed up at the deep,

1

blue sky full of twinkling stars hoping to see one shooting across the sky.

Suddenly, her mind was aggressively pushed open, and she could feel a deliberate harshness enter causing her hands to shake uncontrollably. She pressed her fingers to her forehead feeling the pressure and pain building. It was cold, thick with evil, and hatred. She knew the feel of his thoughts and immediately knew it was Jario before he spoke, "Get ready my sweet Lara. I am coming for you."

Chapter 1

Since Lady Lara's safe return, time had quietly passed for everyone at Evergreen Castle. As far as the Evergreen Army was concerned, it had been too quiet. Jario had not been seen since her kidnapping, and rumors circulated through the surrounding villages that he was making Black Thistle Castle his new fortress. It was common knowledge that Magna had already taken up residence in the castle dungeon. With their merging, there were many at Evergreen that feared a plague of evil could be delivered upon the villages of Alltree Island.

Wagons had been seen hauling supplies from the docks at Echo Bluff Harbor and Cobb Cove through the dirt roadways leading to Black Thistle Castle. Along with the wagons, several men were seen making their way to the castle in hopes of finding work making the much needed repairs. They received a good sum for their work, and word spread fast causing men from other villages to come in search of the much needed wages. Many among the Evergreen Army feared Jario was not only using the men for work, but he could be planning on eventually turning them into an army of deadly vampires.

As each ship docked in the harbor, more and more men arrived seeking work at the castle. Numerous tents and lean-tos were raised each day in the meadow and the forest surrounding the castle. Even though most of the men that came looking for work were honest men wanting to make a good wage for their families, there were a number of men looking to take what they wanted from the shops, homes, and the women of nearby cottages. This caused the Evergreen Army to increase their patrols leaving their own castle more vulnerable. Worried the trouble would spread, Thomas felt the need to send a message of warning to nearby Cumberland Castle. He wanted them to know of the increased trouble that might head their way and to ask for their assistance if matters worsened.

Thomas could hear the usual members of the army going through their practice drills as he approached the Command Center. He stood at the doorway watching Baxter and Frances working with some of the youngest members of the army. New recruits had joined the army after hearing of Lady Lara's kidnapping. She was a favorite among the Echo Bluff village, and they felt the need to repay her frequent help and kindness with their own offer of protection.

Hearing the side door open, Thomas saw Preston, Elda and Tate enter the Command Center along with Will and Oliver. Thomas approached the group knowing they were all here for the meeting in the Council Chamber. He wanted a moment with his brother before the meeting started. Before he could ask Tate to wait, they all stood at attention and saluted with their fists crossed over their chest and the official greeting of My Lord. He appreciated their show of respect, but it was going to take some time to get use to the new title.

Pulling his brother aside, he spoke to the others, "I will meet you in the Council Chamber. I need a moment with Tate."

Tate carefully watched his brother's eyes. He knew the challenges he faced with his blindness and the toll it took on him to pull his vision for long periods of time. He had tried to be his eyes whenever he could to prevent the exhaustion that made Thomas require frequent rest.

"I see you watching my eyes," Thomas said. "This is what I wanted to talk to you about. I am sure you have noticed that my ability to hold my vision has improved since Lara and I have exchanged blood."

"I have noticed a great deal. You still tire from using your vision too long," Tate replied. "You still require a great amount of rest. Rest you avoid."

"Yes, I avoid rest. I need to practice," Thomas snapped, as he interrupted his brother before he could continue to bark at him. "I practice with my sword to improve my ability with my sword. I must continue to practice pulling my vision until I am strong enough to maintain it. It has improved with practice. I can now draw my vision more quickly."

Tate could hear the frustration in his brother's voice, and he took hold of Thomas' shoulders trying to calm him. It was hard not to notice the cloudy film that covered his eyes when he was tired.

"Yes, it is still a struggle if I have used it too often," Thomas conceded. "But, I am happy that it has improved. Brother, you should be happy too." He looked at Tate through his blurry vision and saw the sadness in Tate's eyes. "I have to believe that it will continue to improve, but I need your help to find out if there is a way to undo Velsa's spell. Preferably, without making another bargain with the old hag."

"Do not misunderstand me. I am happy that it has improved. Do not be angry with me. I simply worry about you, brother," Tate replied, as he looked for his brother's understanding. "Have you spoken with the witch, Meadow? Is she able to help you?"

"Yes, she is searching for a loophole that might undo the curse. She will be seeking the witch that resides at Cumberland Castle for help," he responded. "If there is no loophole, I fear I won't be able to protect Lara if I don't have the strength to hold my vision."

"You will always have me and an army to help protect Lady Lara," Tate said. "Never forget that we will be there for you. Besides, you did pretty well without your sight down in the canyon, as I recall."

Thomas nodded but knew his blindness and his persistent overuse of his gift of vision was a weakness. It needed to be corrected soon. With the increase of men and trouble around Black Thistle Castle, he needed his eyesight back and soon.

"Let's get to the Council Chamber before Lady Lara comes looking for us," Tate grinned, as he put his arm around his brother's shoulder and proceeded to lead him to the hallway.

* * *

Everyone was standing behind their chairs when Thomas and Tate entered the Council Chamber. Seeing Lara's expression, he could tell that she was tense. Stepping toward her, he placed a kiss lightly upon her forehead and wrapped an arm around her waist pulling her gently against him. Feeling her body relax, he pulled out the chair for her to take her place next to him. As Thomas took his seat, the council did the same.

"What news of Jario and his new herd of workers?" asked Thomas, as he looked about the room. "I have asked for reports about the increased violence and the number of men employed by Jario."

"We count upwards of fifty men camping around the castle and more arrive every day. They are mostly in the meadow, but a few have camped under the cover of the forest. From a safe distance, we have observed limited weapons. The weapons that we could see were farm picks, long sharpened wooden stakes, and a few men with quivers of arrows. The men do not appear to be trained in fighting," reported Oliver, as he turned to look at Will.

"They are worked from sunrise to sunset and collapse to their blankets shortly after their meager evening meals are eaten," Will added.

"Fights in the tavern have increased, and Zeb has asked for a guard to be present during the evening hours to deter the drunken brawls. Lulu has swung her large pewter tray over a few heads, but it doesn't seem to keep them under control for long," responded Baxter, as he looked at the others around the table for more comments.

"I have been to a few cottages in the farming areas, and folks are keeping their doors and shutter's closed at night. A few cottages have been broken into and robbed of the few precious items they own. One father heard his daughter's screams and found a man trying to rape her. He split the man's head open with a shovel, but the man was able to hobble away. They are becoming more aggressive," Elda said. "I think the ones causing the trouble, for the most part, are probably not the men that Jario has been working to death. The men causing problems are just taking advantage of the numbers of new men in the village. They want to do their dirty work and be hidden amongst the large number of men coming here to work."

Lara sat quietly listening to the reports of the horrible things that were happening to her beloved people. She had waited too long to tell Thomas of Jario's evil intrusion into her mind and simply forced herself to forget about it. Months had passed since then, and fortunately, she had felt nothing from Jario. Since he hadn't returned, it made her feel confident that he would no longer be a threat to her. After hearing of the danger her people faced, she knew she needed to tell Thomas. She knew she should have told Thomas when it happened. She should have told him in private, but she realized it was the right time to let everyone know.

Clearing her throat, Lara spoke when she had everyone's attention, "I have heard from Jario."

Thomas turned and looked at Lara with a stunned expression upon his face. "You what?" Thomas asked. "When did this happen?"

"I have heard from Jario. He forcibly entered my mind some months ago. I felt pure evil and hatred flowing through to me," she replied, with a strong steady voice not wanting to show any fear to the members of the council. "He is still a threat to Evergreen."

"Why didn't you tell me?" asked Thomas, as he lifted her chin so that he could look at her face. "I am sorry I was not there to help you."

"It only lasted a moment, and I am fine. He did not hurt me," she answered him, trying to smile. "He spoke only a few words, but they were meaningful." She paused for a moment and then uttered Jario's message, "Get ready my sweet Lara. I am coming for you."

"He will never have you again, as long as I am able to fight," swore

Thomas. "I will make sure he sees his final death for the harm that he has brought you."

"We will all protect you, Lady Lara," said Tate, as he stood up before the council members. "If necessary, we will forfeit our lives to protect you."

Hearing Tate's honorable words, the entire council stood to affirm Tate's vow. Thomas looked among the council members and knew that they were true to Evergreen and to Lady Lara. They were all his trusted friends, and their allegiance meant the world to him.

"Preston, put together a plan to curtail the violence within the village and do it quickly. Our people cannot suffer any longer," Thomas ordered. "If you feel our forces are spread too thin, we have assurances from Cumberland Castle that they will assist us in any way we need help. They don't want to see this spread in their direction."

"Yes, My Lord," responded Preston.

"Let us meet back here in two days to discuss the plans," Thomas said, as he helped Lara stand. "Until then, be watchful and report any signs of Jario or Magna to Preston."

Dismissing the council, Thomas led Lara back to their bedchamber. He held her hand tightly as he brought it to his mouth to kiss her fingers numerous times before they reached their chamber door. Grasping the iron handle and opening the door, he scooped Lara up in his arms and carried her into their bedchamber. Kicking the door closed with the heel of his boot, he made his way toward their bed.

"I think I should give you something else to think about," whispered Thomas, as he softly kissed her neck just below her ear. "I only want thoughts of me loving you lingering in your mind."

* * *

As Tate started to walk back to the Command Center, he saw Niobe running toward him. "Sir, come quickly," she panted, sounding out of breath from running. "Your lady friend, Gavenia, is awake. Thank the stars and the heavens, she is finally awake."

Tate quickly followed Niobe down the hallway to the Healing Room. Reaching the doorway, he could see Gavenia sitting up with her back against the frame of the cot. Flora sat by her side holding a cup of broth as she helped her take small sips from a wooden spoon. Careful not to scare her, he walked slowly to the foot of the cot. Watching her eyes, he looked for any signs of recognition.

"Gavenia, how are you feeling?" he asked, as he tilted his head and bent slightly trying to make eye contact with her.

She looked up at Tate, clearly hearing his voice, but she quickly returned to the warm broth that Flora offered to her.

"How is she?" asked Tate, as he stepped around the side of the cot and sat down upon the linen covers.

Gavenia drew her feet up moving her knees against her chest. She did not seem to be afraid of him, but he sensed that she did not want him to touch her.

"She has only been awake for a short time and has not spoken a single word," replied Flora. "I sent Niobe to bring you here; I wanted to see if she recognized you. Clearly, she does not remember you. It will be awhile before we know how much damage has been done to her mind. Her body is healing well, but wounds of the mind take much longer to heal."

"Is there anything that I can do to help," asked Tate, feeling helpless. "I will do anything. You need only ask me."

"As long as she will allow you in the room, you may visit her," answered Flora. "Do not pressure her into trying to remember you. Let it happen on its own. Understand that she may never remember you. If you cause her distress, I will ask you to leave and refrain from seeing her. Have I made myself clear?"

Tate felt the sting of Flora's words. If she remembered Tate, she would probably remember Magna and everything that happened in the dungeon. She would remember the things Magna made him do to her. He decided he would be careful with the things he said to her and wait for however long it took for her to become completely well. He would eventually have to apologize for his actions, but that could wait. He stood from the cot and took a seat on the stool in the corner of the room. He just wanted to be near her and be there to help, if he could.

Flora fed Gavenia the last of the broth. Seeing the cup was empty, Gavenia pushed her body back down upon the cot with her head on the pillow. Flora tucked the bed linens around her, and Gavenia closed her eyes to sleep. Tate watched as her chest rose with each breath. He was grateful that he no longer feared that her breathing would stop. She looked much better than she did when he brought her to the Healing Room. Her skin was pale, and the numerous bite marks inflicted by Magna and Jario were healing. They would scar, but he hoped for her sake, they would fade along with the memory of how she received them.

Knowing that she was sleeping, Tate stood and headed toward the doorway. He turned back to look at her. She was beautiful. Her skin was very fair and a few freckles were sprinkled across her nose and onto her cheeks. He had seen the green of her eyes before she closed them to sleep, and he was sure they would be as bright as emeralds once she was completely well. The wounds on her scalp were healing and once her red hair grew back, she would be even lovelier.

He so wanted to touch her once before he left. He quietly stepped forward. Cautiously, he brought his hand to her cheek, and with the back of his hand, he lightly touched her soft skin. Instantly, he felt warmth race through his arm to his chest. He saw a slight tremble of her body telling him that she had felt it too. Pulling his hand back quickly, he felt the warmth slowly fade. He smiled thankful that the warmth he had felt before had not vanished. They definitely had some kind of a connection. A connection that he wanted to last. A connection that he would protect with his life.

Chapter 2

Jario watched Buck supervising the men cutting blocks from a large stone that had been hauled out of the Canyon of Obscurity. He stood in the shadows of one of the chambers in the upper portion of Black Thistle Castle. It was one of the few chambers that had not been demolished by the War of the Witches or fallen to ruins after decades of neglect. The rebuilding was a slow process, and he was anxious to get it completed so he could direct his focus back on the destruction of Evergreen.

The drawbridge had been rebuilt, and it was sturdy enough to pull the wagons full of blocks across it into the courtyard. The dungeon's cells were all intact, but they required the skill of blacksmiths to repair the rusted cell doors and add new locks. He had hoped for more skilled workers when he sent out word of his need to repair the castle. Unfortunately, he had received mostly farmers in need of coin.

Jario turned and took in the view of his chamber. He had made sure that the stone floor had been polished, and the black metal chandelier had been cleaned and oiled. The huge bed and windows had been dressed with brocade and velvet he had purchased from the merchants that had arrived in the harbor. He continued to gaze about the chamber as he walked with his arm outstretched running his fingers along the rich wood panels that lined the walls. This chamber was much grander than his chamber at Evergreen, but he was now the Master of Black Thistle Castle, and he deserved grand accommodations.

As his eyes lingered on the lavish appointments of his bedchamber, he noticed a small stone resting on the floor. Bending to pick it up, he found it was set deep into the stones of the floor. Curious of its use, he walked about the walls looking for any sign of a hidden door using his hands to feel for any seam or gap in each panel. Finding none, he pressed the stone firmly with the toe of his boot. Hearing a deep groan, he watched as a panel within the wall slowly began to move toward him and swing wide into the chamber. Stunned, he moved forward and pressed his hand against the frame of the open door.

"What is this?" Jario gasped, as he peered into the dark space. "I have stumbled upon a secret chamber. Is this where others sat hidden during the War of the Witches?"

After securing the door with a heavy chair, he pulled a burning torch from its iron bracket. As he made his way inside the dark chamber, his nostrils were greeted by its cold musty scent of old wood and leather. Jario knew that the enclosed space had not been blessed with a fresh breeze in decades and probably longer. He surmised that no one had seen the chamber since the War of the Witches.

It was a small space but large enough to walk around freely. The stone walls were lined with numerous thick wooden shelves. He noticed that upon each shelf stood several wooden chests. Large leather bound books and rolled parchments were tucked into the narrow spaces between each of the chests to keep them from falling. A large map hung precariously by one spike and swayed as Jario moved about the chamber. Stacked against the walls, he found more leather bound books of all sizes covered in cobwebs. A vast display of Longswords and daggers decorated with gemstones were hung upon the walls.

Holding the burning torch, he looked about the chamber for a place to stand the torch's base. Turning back toward the door, he saw an iron bracket and carefully inserted the base of the torch, making sure it was secure. Having the freedom to explore the contents of the chamber, he opened a wooden chest to find it full of gold coins. One by one, he opened each chest and discovered each chest contained the same. Realizing he had stumbled upon a fortune, Jario began to laugh as he moved around the chamber touching each chest of gold. The prior ruler had carefully hidden his gold coins, and Jario had been lucky enough to find them.

Jario knew that he needed to keep the discovery of this room a complete secret. He did not trust Magna and feared that Gusty or Buck might give him a final death to obtain the gold for themselves. He looked about the chamber for something similar to the stone set into the floor that had allowed him to open the panel. If the panel should close while he was inside, he needed to be able to reopen it.

Surely, someone would have created a way to exit the room if the door should close by accident, he thought.

Searching the floor for any stone that would appear to be a mechanism for the door, he could not find anything that resembled the raised stone he had stepped on to release the door. He began picking up each chest and carefully moving the daggers from side to side. The release appeared to be well hidden. Frustrated, he leaned against the stone wall and felt something jab him in the back. As he did, he heard the same deep groan along with the scraping of the chair he had placed in front of the door. Quickly, stepping out of the chamber and pulling the chair away from the door, he watched as the panel closed, becoming completely invisible. Knowing where the panel was, he still could not see anything that indicated that it existed. The opening and closing of the door left no trace of its movement upon the floor. It was indeed, completely hidden. Rubbing his hands together from excitement, he again stepped upon the stone to open the panel.

Back inside the chamber, he felt safe since finding the additional stone release embedded in the wall. Feeling more relaxed, he began to examine the treasures he had found with more scrutiny. Taking his time, he ran his hand over each dagger. He had started to count the gemstones until he lost count due to his excitement and their great number. However, one simple longsword drew his attention. A single ruby was secured within the leather bindings of its hilt. He noticed its blade held engraving that seemed to appear and disappear with the flickering light of the torch.

Moving to allow the light to completely expose the engraving, he studied the words for a moment before he said, "Fuaim na Cumhacta." Jario searched his mind for the meaning of the words. "I know this language. It means Sound of Power. A simple sword like this must have been a gift to a young man. It isn't sturdy enough to be a warrior's sword."

As Jario ran his finger over the engraving, the longsword seemed to hum. Disturbed by the sudden delicate sound, he stepped away and rubbed his palms against each other. Shaking the sound from his mind, he looked about the small chamber and realized he had suddenly become a very wealthy vampire. With wealth, he could buy power. With power, he could destroy Evergreen.

Turning to leave the chamber, he noticed a small wooden table set against the stone wall hidden among the shadows. The pedestal was hand carved with the heads of wild boars that were set among large thistles. There in the middle of the table, almost hidden within the darkness, sat a black chest with a small gold clasp. Lifting the clasp and opening the lid to the chest, he found a dagger encrusted with rubies secured in the thick black fabric that lined the lid of the chest. Tucked in its bottom was a folded parchment sealed with dark red sealing wax. He lifted the aged parchment, and as he did, the delicate seal broke into several small pieces. The temperature in the room began to drop. A shiver slithered up his back as he heard a sound similar to a deep moan or sigh fill the chamber. It caused him to look over his shoulder for someone that might have entered his bedchamber unannounced. No one was present, but he still did not feel that he was alone.

I am letting all this gold coin play with my nerves, he thought, as he turned his focus back to the parchment within his hands.

The parchment was yellowed with age, and he carefully opened it to find some words written in beautiful calligraphy.

Remove the chains, Unbind the pain, Release the fear, Retrieve Gautier

Without thinking, Jario read the words out loud, and as he did, the torch within the chamber began to flare wildly. The chamber's temperature began to drop even more. Feeling very uncomfortable, he placed the parchment back into the black chest and closed the lid. He moved quickly to press the stone within the wall to close the door. Taking the torch from its bracket, he stepped out of the chamber just before the panel closed.

With a sigh of relief, he placed the torch back within the chamber's bracket and took a moment to think about what he had found. He smiled, as he made his way to the bedchamber door. Reaching for the large iron handle, he again heard the groan of the hidden chamber's door. He turned starring in confusion at the door as it opened on its own. Taking a step back towards the open panel, he suddenly stopped frozen in place. His mouth gapped open as he watched a tall man dressed completely in black step from the room into his chamber.

"I am Gautier, and you have released me from a binding spell," Gautier announced with a raspy voice, as he walked to the center of the bedchamber. He slowly turned and looked about the space that surrounded him. Looking back at Jario, he raised his hands as if her were confused. "Where is my beloved? Where is my Kayleigh?" Hearing no response from Jario, fear and then anger crossed Gautier's face as he screamed, "Where is she? What have you done with her?"

*   *   *

Magna had stormed down to her dungeon after arguing with Jario over an attractive young man she had been distracting from his work. She had been warned to stay away from the men working in the castle, but Magna wasn't good at taking orders. She would never be good at taking orders from Jario. After all, she had made Black Thistle Castle her home long before Jario arrived.

Since discovering the castle as a child, Magna grew up walking among the ruins of the castle pretending to be a wicked queen commanding torture and death to all that betrayed her. The black thistles surrounding the castle seemed to come alive when she walked among them as she caressed their thorns with the tips of her fingers. As a young woman, she loved the way the castle made her feel and decided, then and there, to someday make it her home if it was ever rebuilt. It was after her turning that she ran from Evergreen and hid within the dungeons of Black Thistle Castle. As she leaned against the dungeon wall, memories of her turning began to fill her mind as if it were yesterday.

It was at this castle that she met the vampire that turned her. He was standing in the courtyard watching her run among the thistles and merrily laughing. He was mesmerized as he observed the thistles' thorns playfully piercing her arms and hands leaving droplets of blood upon her skin and the ground.

Seeing a long shadow stretch across the courtyard entrance, Magna stepped onto the drawbridge to see who had invaded her private domain. Raising her eyes, she tried to look up at his face. The brightness of the sun had made it difficult to see anything, and she had been forced to lower her eyes and look upon the man's black leather boots. Realizing the sun caused her eyes great difficulty, he kindly moved to block the sun from her eyes. Thankful for his thoughtfulness, she looked up and noticed his pale skin and his black wavy hair that hung to his elbows. The black tunic he wore was open and hung loosely over his tight breeches.

"You have entered my castle without permission," Magna boldly said, as she crossed her arms over her chest trying not to show any fear. "Who are you, and why are you here?"

"My name is Francisco, but you may call me Franco. I have come to rest in the quiet of the castle dungeon," he replied. "I did not know that a beautiful queen had already claimed it for her own. Shall I make my leave, or would you be so kind as to show me your kingdom?"

Magna smiled as she dropped her arms to her side. She straightened her back and raised her chin trying to appear regal. Magna loved that he made her feel regal.

"I did not expect visitors today, but I will gladly show you my castle" she replied.

He offered his arm as she slipped her arm through his and headed toward the large hole in the wall made by the crumbling stones. He listened to her tell him about finding the castle and her dreams to live there one day with a huge army that would do her bidding. He could hear the evil in her voice and delighted in her descriptions of torture for those who did not follow her commands.

Taking the last few steps leading to the dungeon, she let go of his arm to reach for a torch mounted high upon the wall. Seeing that she could not easily reach it, he lifted her so she could grasp the base of the wooden torch. Holding it high above her head, Magna showed him the cells and the chains that hung from the walls. A spiked table sat in the middle of one of the cells, and she traced the spikes with her fingertips as she walked alongside the table.

"You have seen all of my castle and the nasty dungeon," she said, as she raised her arm to point at the spikes. "If you would like to rest here within the dungeon, there is a feather cushion upon the floor. I brought it here so that I would have a place to sit when it rains."

"That would do nicely," Franco replied. "Would you sit with me for a while? I have not had the company of a queen's conversation for such a long time."

She nodded and walked to the cushion in the corner of the dimly lit space facing the cells. Handing the torch to Franco, he placed it in a bracket found near a cell door. It offered a dim light in the corner, but it still provided enough darkness to easily rest. He helped her sit and watched as she straightened her skirt. He was trying to control his need for blood and didn't want to scare her away suddenly. She had let the fox into the hen house, and he fully intended on feasting on all it had to offer.

"You have listened to me," she said, giving him a playful smile. "Tell me about your desires."

He turned to look at her face and saw that her cheeks were blushing after realizing the double meaning of her wording. He could smell her arousal, as well as, her uneasiness, and knew that he needed to be careful.

"My boots are muddy, and I don't want to get mud upon your feather cushion," he said, as he stood and removed his boots. He pulled his tunic over his head and folded it neatly placing it on the stone floor alongside the cushion. Sitting back down, he leaned back upon his elbows and pretended to yawn.

"I guess I am more tired than I thought," Franco said, as he continued to yawn.

Magna turned and looked back at Franco. She knew that she should leave him to rest, but she was fascinated by him and had been secretly pretending he was a visiting king that had come to court her for marriage.

If only he would kiss me once, she thought, as her cheeks flushed again.

"I will let you rest, but first I must give you a kiss good night. It is the custom here in this castle to kiss visitors good night," she said, as she knelt and leaned over him and brushed his lips gently with a kiss. "Good night King Franco, it has been a pleasure visiting with you this evening."

Not wanting her leave, he decided to play along with her little game.

"I have travelled far to find you and have come to ask for your hand in marriage,"

15

he said, wondering if she would continue to play the game. "It would make me very happy if we could be wed tonight."

Magna blushed, but she was enjoying the game of pretend. She stood and put her hands on her hips giving him a frown.

"Is that a proper proposal?" she asked. "My future king would stand and get down on one knee while professing his love for me before asking me to marry."

Franco immediately stood and knelt down on one knee. He removed a gold ring from his finger as he asked, "My beautiful Queen of Black Thistle Castle, would you do me the great honor of joining with me in marriage and accept my love, as well as, my protection for you and your castle?"

Magna smiled and nodded her head as she replied, "Yes King Franco, I will accept your proposal of marriage."

He placed the gold ring upon her thumb and kissed the back of her hand as he inhaled her scent of smoldering coals. He smiled as he stood and began to recite, "I, King Franco, take you as my bride. I will protect you and love you forever more."

Grinning from ear to ear, Magna responded, "I, Queen Magna, take you as my husband. I will protect you and love you forever more."

He leaned down and held her face between his hands and kissed her. She swayed from his kiss and kept her eyes closed hoping for another. Kissing her again, he could feel her heart flutter with excitement. Moving her carefully back to the cushion, he picked her up and placed her back against the smooth surface. He leaned down and stroked her face gently with his hand and kissed her again. This time she opened her mouth taking his searching tongue. He placed his body next to hers and moved his hand up and down her arm as he looked into her eyes.

Softly he said, using his compulsion, "We are married, my Queen, and you will act as my bride in every way."

After reveling in the perfection of her nakedness and divulging his wicked desires to her, he took his time exploring and tasting every part of her. He felt the barrier between them and heard her whimper as it gave way to the firmness of his body. The rush he felt with the fulfillment of his release was wonderful the first time but, utterly marvelous as he took her every way he could over and over throughout the night. As he prepared to turn her, he looked at her beautiful naked body and kissed her one last time.

She woke finding him gone. Blood ran from her wrists, her neck and her breasts. Feeling the terrible soreness from between her thighs, she saw the blood and began to cry as she felt every bit of his betrayal. She had been a fool to trust him. He had taken her blood and her virginity. A strange fire began to swell within her throat. Clawing at her neck, she realized that he had turned her. Closing her eyes, she made a vow that Franco would see his final death by her hand. She would seek torture on every man she could find, and it would be a delicious revenge. She would hate them all.

Frantically she dressed herself and ran from the dungeon. Her father would help her like he had helped her sister, Lara. She would control the madness and use it as a *weapon to seek her revenge.*

Feeling tears swell in her eyes, Magna remembered every detail of the game of pretend that she had shared with Franco. If she ever saw him again, she would make sure he felt her revenge over and over again until she gave him his final death. Wiping the tears from her face, she straightened her back as she tried to forget.

She was pulled away suddenly from her memories, hearing the chains in the small cell rattle against the stone wall. Confused, she stepped toward the cell. A dim light appeared, and then she saw a translucent vision of a woman standing against the rough stones with heavy cuffs about her wrists. Magna stood utterly bewildered as she stared at the woman.

"Where did she come from?" she whispered.

Looking to see if any other cell was occupied, she stepped closer to the vision. She knew she had not restrained anyone in the cells, and Jario would have told her if he was beginning to take prisoners.

Magna watched as the vision of the woman solidified, and she struggled to lift her heavily restrained arms. Tears ran down her face as she looked about the dungeon cell as if she didn't recognize anything around her. Seeing Magna, she took a step forward causing the cuffs to suddenly fall from her wrists and swing back crashing against the stone wall. Magna stepped toward the bars of the cell feeling a strange need to offer her help. She could see the fear in the woman's eyes, and then without warning, the woman screamed, "Gautier!"

* * *

Jario backed up against the wooden door. At once, Gautier had Jario by the throat with his feet dangling two feet off the ground. The look on Gautier's face was that of uncontrollable rage.

He looked into Jario's eyes and asked again, "Where is my Kayleigh? I will tear you limb from limb if you have harmed her."

"I do not know the woman that you speak of," Jario managed to choke out, as Gautier's hands relaxed enough for him to speak. "There are only a few of us in the castle and none by the name you have given."

Gautier pulled his hand back and watched Jario drop. Jario felt his boots and then his knees hit the floor. Jario reached for his neck and began rubbing the bruises left behind from Gautier's strong grip. Gautier paced anxiously about the chamber as he continued to stare at Jario. Trying to calm himself, he moved to the window. Gazing out into the darkness, he realized that time had changed all that he remembered. The castle was in ruins, and the War of the Witches had ended.

"Who won the War of the Witches?" Gautier asked, not turning to look at Jario. "It was during the war that a spell was cast upon me, binding me to that chamber."

"The legends, told by many, say that Velsa won the war," Jario coughed, still rubbing his neck. "Were you the Lord of this castle during the war?"

"Velsa?" Gautier repeated the name Jario had used, as he closed his eyes searching his memories. "I remember that old hag. She is not to be trusted, and my binding is proof of it." He paced back and forth in front of the window with his hand held to his brow. "You must forgive me, my memories seem to be muddled and are offering me some pain when I search them. To answer your question, no. This was my brother's castle. He was a human and must have died in the war along with many others. If not then, he has surely passed by now." He stopped and stood still as he gazed out the window. "I lived here in the castle with my beloved, Kayleigh. I fear she is lost to me, as well."

"As you can see, I am trying to repair the castle," Jario said, hoping not to raise fury into Gautier. "I plan to live in this castle and build an army."

Gautier turned and declared, "I owe you a great debt for breaking the binding spell. I have the power to help you restore the castle."

"What power is this?" Jario asked, unsure of a man wielding power, he took a few steps back toward the door.

"Power beyond anything you can imagine," Gautier smirked, as he waved his hand and made a fire appear within the hearth. "If you have not figured it out, I am a warlock. I have made a few witches angry over the years, Velsa in particular. She has a quick temper and felt scorned by me. She was the reason why I found myself a subject of her binding spell."

Jario listened carefully to his offer of help to restore the castle. He was hesitant to make any bargains after his run in with Balgair, but this could put him in a position to destroy Evergreen and capture Lady Lara.

"Is this power something that you can teach me?" asked Jario. "I have need of revenge for an injustice done to me."

"I can relate to the revenge of injustice. I, myself, feel the need for revenge. However, once I know that I can trust you, vampire, we can discuss lessons," Gautier replied, with a smirk. "Yes, I know that you are a vampire. Let's walk outside. I need to feel the night air. It has been quite stuffy where I have been held."

Jario turned and reached for the door. He heard the sound of Gautier's boots close behind him. Jario grabbed the iron handle and

18

pulled the door open for Gautier to exit the chamber. As Gautier took a step forward, a terrifying scream was heard echoing through the stone hallways. Gautier turned to look at Jario. Frozen in place, he heard his name pierce his ears, and then felt the strength of it slam against his chest knocking his feet out from under him.

"The dungeon," shouted Jario. "It must have come from the dungeon."

The two men ran through the hallways and down the flight of stone steps to the dungeon. Stepping into its dim light, Jario saw Magna standing in front of a cell. She turned when she heard them approaching and lifted her hand to point toward the cell.

"She just appeared out of thin air," Magna said, as her voice cracked more from surprise than fear. "She was bound by chains until they fell from her wrists. I have no idea where she came from."

Looking in the direction that Magna pointed, Jario saw a woman standing in the middle of the cell. She was pale and thin with long curly hair the color of flax and wore an ivory dressing gown that was not of the current style. Hearing the movement within the dungeon, the woman looked up and immediately held up her arms.

"Gautier! Oh, my love. You have found me," she cried, as tears ran down her face. "I was alone, and it was so very dark and cold. Gautier, I could not find you."

He rushed to the cell as his hand waved and the cell door flew open crashing against the iron bars. Pulling her to his body, she rested her face against his chest as tears continued to stream down her face. They stood embraced as they seemed to melt against each other. Gautier held her tightly with one arm around her waist as he caressed her hair with his other hand and softly repeated, "Kayleigh! Kayleigh! My sweet Kayleigh."

Chapter 3

The afternoon sun was hidden behind the tall trees surrounding Evergreen, and the heat of the day was slowly giving way to the cool afternoon breeze that blew in from the harbor. Expecting the arrival of Lady Lara, Tolin led her cherished horses out to the new larger pen for exercise. He had brushed the dirt and mud from their coats and used his special brush with soft bristles to make their coats shine. Their hoofs were cleaned and polished, and great attention was given to the combing and brushing of their manes and tails. Lady Lara had not made a visit to the stables to see Mona and her colt, Arrow, since the night she was taken. It was important to Tolin, as the Horse Master of Evergreen, to have the horses look their best for Lady Lara's long awaited visit.

Lara made her way down the stone steps. She was anxious to see how much Arrow had grown since her last visit. Stopping by the kitchen to get a few treats for the horses, she saw that Charlotte had thoughtfully left a bowl of carrots and green beans on the corner of the wooden table for her. Stuffing the treats into the pockets of her dress, she made her way to the exercise pen.

She could see Arrow running and kicking in the clover that covered most of the pen's ground. He was a frisky colt, and she looked forward to watching him grow. As she reached the pen, Mona stopped her grazing and made her way toward Lara. She lifted her nose above the railings and nudged Lara's cheek.

"I have missed you too, sweet Mona," Lara quietly whispered, as she put her hands on either side of Mona's head kissing her nose. "I have brought you a treat."

She put her hand in her pocket and pulled out a carrot. Mona stepped back and slowly lowered her head in a bow. As she raised her head, Lara offered the carrot and watched as Mona carefully took it from her hand.

Hearing someone coming from the stone steps behind her, Lara turned to see Niobe and Gavenia walking toward her. Niobe held her hand as they walked slowly toward the pen. Gavenia was still pale and very thin, but Flora expected her to start gaining weight now that she was eating small meals.

"Lady Lara, we decided to join you," said Niobe, as she made a small curtsy. "I asked Gavenia if she would like to visit the horses, and she nodded her head that she would. She still hasn't decided to speak, but she responds to questions with her head."

"It is nice to have some company," replied Lara. "Come stand by me at the railings. I will share my carrots and beans with you."

Lara pulled a few beans and a carrot from her pocket and placed them on the palm of her hand offering them to Gavenia. Gavenia looked at them and carefully took them making sure not to touch Lady Lara's hand. To show her how to feed Mona, Lara placed a bean on the palm of her hand and offered it over the railing as she watched Mona nibble it carefully from her palm.

"Would you like to try?" asked Lara.

Without hesitation, Gavenia nodded and placed a bean on the palm of her hand and then offered the treat to Mona. Mona moved over to face her and raised her head over the railing and carefully took the bean. Hearing the crunching noise, Gavenia smiled and took another bean to offer her another treat. Seeing Mona take it again, Gavenia stepped closer to the railing. Reaching her hand out, she tried to touch Mona's head. Mona backed up a few steps, and Gavenia's smile quickly left her face.

"Mona, come forward," Lara said. "Gavenia would like to be your friend. She wants to touch your pretty face. She will not harm you."

Mona stepped forward toward the railing and put her nose over the wooden rails in front of Gavenia. Seeing Lady Lara nod her approval, Gavenia raised her hand slowly and stroked the side of Mona's head. Leaning forward, she pressed her face against Mona's head and continued to stroke her face closing her eyes. Seeing Gavenia's affection for Mona, Niobe smiled and winked at Lady Lara.

They all stood at the railings for a while watching Mona graze and Arrow run and kick his hind legs until he became tired and began to nuzzle his mother for milk. Afraid the outing may have been too much for Gavenia, Niobe motioned back to the castle.

"It was nice of you to visit me and my horses," Lara said. "You are welcome to visit anytime. If you don't mind, I will walk back to the Healing Room with you."

Gavenia nodded and took hold of Niobe's hand as they walked back to the castle. As they reached the stone steps, Gavenia turned toward the trees. She lifted her arm and pointed to the birds fluttering among the branches. Releasing Niobe's hand, she started to run toward the trees, but she stumbled and fell upon her hands and knees. Lara and Niobe ran to her side. They bent down to help Gavenia stand, but they realized she was struggling to take a breath.

"Run and fetch Flora," ordered Lara, as she stroked Gavenia's back. "Please hurry, Niobe."

"I am here with you, Gavenia. Do not be afraid," whispered Lara. "We will help you. Flora is coming."

Flora ran down the steps hearing Gavenia choking and gasping for breath. She knelt beside her and placed one hand under her chin. With the other hand, she rubbed small warm circles upon her heaving back until her breathing calmed.

"Can you stand?" asked Flora.

Gavenia nodded, and Flora took her arm to help her stand. Her face was flushed and a fine bead of perspiration covered her forehead. She swayed slightly and leaned against Flora for support.

"I will take her back to her bed to rest," Flora said, as she made eye contact with Lara and then directed her sight to the ground littered with feathers.

"The excitement of the horses must have been too much for her first outing," said Lara, as she stroked Gavenia's arm. "We can sit in the courtyard and drink some of Charlotte's mint tea, when you feel better. It is quiet there, and I am sure you will enjoy the fountain and the beautiful flowers."

Gavenia gave Lady Lara a weak smile as they walked back to the castle. Looking over her shoulder at the trees, Gavenia sighed and leaned against Flora. Bending down, Lara picked up the feathers that littered the ground and headed off to find Woodward.

* * *

Lara gently knocked upon Woodward's door. As she waited for him to answer, she looked down at the feathers she held in her hand. The door opened and Woodward smiled, as he bowed and placed his fist over his heart.

"My Lady, what brings you to my door this evening?" he asked, as he stepped aside for her to enter. "Please take the seat by the fire. The night air has started to cool with the fall season upon us."

Lara stepped into the small cottage and sat down in the chair he had offered. She watched Woodward close the door and walk to the table to retrieve the dented tea kettle.

"I was just about to make some tea. Would you have a cup with me?" Woodward asked, as he picked up the kettle. "Charlotte brought me some of her mint tea with the assurance that I would enjoy it."

Lara smiled, as she thought about Charlotte, but shook her head, "No thank you, I won't be staying long. I have come to ask you to identify the feathers in my hand. I have not seen them before, and I was sure you would be able to tell me what bird they came from."

Woodward put down the kettle and took the feathers from Lady Lara's hand. He stepped closer to the fire for better light and turned the feathers over in his hand as he examined them.

"I believe that these are from a Peregrine hawk or falcon, My Lady," he responded. "It is a beautiful hawk with a white face and speckled chest feathers. It is also very swift in flight and may be the fastest bird I have ever seen. Where did you find these?"

"I found them near the new exercise pen," she replied. "This hawk would not harm the colt, would it?"

"No, My Lady," he answered, handing the feathers back to her. "They prey upon birds and bats. Sometimes they snag a duck, but I have never seen them try to feast upon a colt or horse. Is that your worry?"

"It was a worry, but you have put that to rest," she said, as she stood and took a step toward the door. "I will leave you to enjoy your fire and cup of mint tea. I promise to visit you again soon and take advantage of your offer of hospitality. For now, I must go. Have a good evening, Woodward."

"I look forward to it, My Lady," he replied, as he walked her to the door and pulled it open.

"Me too," Lara responded.

"My Lady, I am glad you returned safely back to Evergreen," he said, with sincerity in his voice. "We were all worried for you."

"I am glad to be home too," she said, as she placed her hand upon his arm to show her appreciation. "I thank you for your kind words. Again, good evening."

"Good evening," he replied, as he watched her walk down the path back to the castle.

Thinking of Charlotte, he leaned out the door hoping to see her bringing him some more tea. Glancing at the rear entrance to the castle, he spied the golden glow of the candles in the kitchen window and sighed as he closed the door.

Chapter 4

Lulu was slamming a pewter tray across a man's head and giving a few others a piece of her mind when Tate and Elda entered the tavern. Taking hold of the recipient's arm, Elda pulled him away from a man that had blood running from the corner of his mouth and had a bruise forming on his cheek.

"If you want to fight, you do it outside the tavern," shouted Elda. "This is a place of business, and I'm making it my business to keep this kind of thing from happening."

The man flung his elbow away from Elda and sneered, "A sweet little wench like you is gonna make me stop? You can try. Me will be bending you over this here table showing you all my appreciation before you be stopping me."

Elda looked closely at the brut. He had need of a shave, and it was clear he had not bathed in a long time, if ever. A scar next to his eye and one thick scar on his neck let her know that he frequently settled disagreements with a fight. She had handled men like him before and knew he was too drunk to put up much of a fight.

A few regulars in the tavern starting laughing. They had seen Elda's vampire strength before and knew she could handle him with one hand tied behind her back. The man stepped forward and grabbed Elda's arm. She took hold of his wrist and began to squeeze as she backed towards the tavern door. Tate pulled the door open for her as she gave him a wink and continued to back up until she was outside. Closing the door, Tate headed for the bar. As he did, a man's howling could be heard coming from outside and then silence stilled the air. The next sound came as Elda opened the tavern door. Closing it behind her, she slapped her hands against one another and asked, "Anyone else have an issue with my "No Fighting" request?"

Winking at a few of the regulars, Elda looked about the tavern directing her attention to the men she did not recognize. They quickly closed their gaping mouths and lowered their eyes. Satisfied, she made her way to Lulu.

"Are you alright?" Elda asked her, as she took her arm. "I will be spending some time here keeping these men under control for you. Thomas knows about the trouble the new arrivals are causing, and he wants it stopped."

"Thank you," Lulu replied. "I can usually get their attention by swinging my tray over their head, but tonight there were too many wanting to cause trouble. I will be in need of several new trays if this continues."

Guiding Lulu safely back to the bar, Tate handed Elda a large cup of ale. He looked back across the room trying to memorize the faces of the men that were involved in the scuffle. He was sure that this wouldn't be the end of it, but he hoped that the word would get back to the others that fighting would not be tolerated in the tavern.

* * *

Cummings made his way back to the meadow and crawled under his shelter holding his broken wrist. He wouldn't be able to work with only one hand and no work meant no coins for food or ale. He was just having a little fun with that wench, and she had ruined everything. She had embarrassed him in front of a room full of men. Once he could pick up a dagger, he would make sure it landed between her shoulder blades while he pressed himself against her bare backside. Satisfied with his hatred for the wench, he picked up his blanket to cover himself from the night air and noticed a man wandering through the tents.

Buck was making the rounds through the small shelters. Most of the men were exhausted and had fallen asleep the second their heads hit their blankets. Seeing Cummings was still awake, he stepped over the sleeping men and bent down facing the man huddled under the tattered canvas.

"Why aren't you sleeping? You will have a long day tomorrow," Buck asked, as he spotted the man's swollen wrist.

"Me just got back from a tavern fight," he said, knowing that was a half-truth. "Me thinks me done got me wrist broke."

"You aren't much good to us if you can't work," Buck replied, as he grabbed the man's wrist to see if it was really broken.

Wincing in pain, Cummings hollered, "Me done told you. Me done got me a broken wrist. Me be saying the truth!"

"I will heal it, but do not tell anyone that I have helped you," Buck said, as he looked over his shoulder to see if anyone was listening. He took his dagger and sliced his wrist. As the blood began to swell, he forced his wrist toward Cummings. "Drink. It will heal your wrist."

"Are you crazy in the head," Cummings said, as he scooted away from Buck. "Me will not be drinking your blood."

"Suit yourself," said Buck, as he stood. "I was trying to help you, but I see my offer of help is not accepted. You are the crazy one. Your refusal will leave you in pain for a good number of days and without coins."

Buck started to walk away, but stopped when he heard Cummings signal him to wait. Returning to the lean-to, he again knelt down looking at the man.

"Have you changed your mind?" asked Buck.

"Are you a vampire?" Cummings asked, with a quiver to his voice.

"Yes. It is well-known around this village that vampires live among the humans. I can help you heal with my blood, or if you prefer, I can turn you into a vampire. The choice is yours. Pain, healing or power is what I can offer you. You choose," replied Buck, as he continued to kneel waiting for a response from Cummings.

"Healing now is what me be needing," said Cummings. "Me be thinking on your offer, but it fears me some."

Buck cut his healed wrist and offered the blood to Cummings. Cummings crept closer and closed his eyes not wanting to see the blood that was about to enter his mouth. He wasn't sure he trusted Buck, but he wanted the wrist to heal. Opening his mouth, he covered Buck's wrist and drank the bitter liquid. After a few moments, Buck pulled his wrist away and stood staring down at Cummings.

"Sleep, in the morning your wrist will be healed, and I expect a full day of work from you in return," Buck sternly barked. "If I find you making trouble, you will end up feeling more pain than a tavern fight can offer."

Cummings nodded, and he pulled his blanket up around his shoulders and closed his eyes. He would think more on the offer of becoming a vampire and getting back at the wench that had broken his wrist.

Chapter 5

The ironsmith finished repairing the last cell door and handed Magna the keys to the cells and the restraints. They were lucky to find a skilled ironworker amongst the men camped outside the castle, and he had accepted the offer of a permanent place at the castle for himself and his family. She smirked as she walked to the far side of the dungeon and hung the heavy ring of keys upon a spike that was embedded in the stone wall. The cells were finally finished, and Magna was ready to fill them.

Making her way up to the main level of the castle, she could see that the entry hall walls had been repaired. Men were hoisting the large iron candelabra into place, and the missing entry door had been replaced using the remains of broken beams that had fallen from the ceiling. Moonlight was reflecting on the stone floor through the few small stained glass panes that had survived the war.

Hearing voices coming from the Grand Hall, Magna pushed the door the rest of the way open and found Jario and Gautier standing in the middle of the hall. As she entered the large hall, her senses caught the scent of the men installing the iron brackets to hold the torches around the room. Closing her eyes, she inhaled deeply feeling the need to sample their blood. Her eyes drifted over their bare chests making her tongue moisten her upper lip.

Catching Magna's eyes drifting over the men and her change in direction, Jario excused himself as he made his way quickly to Magna's side.

"I warned you not to bother the men," Jario scolded Magna. "I meant it, Magna. I will not stand for your games. There is a great amount of work to be completed, and I don't want you in the way."

He took her by the arm and started to walk toward Gautier. He felt her struggle against his hold, but kept walking away from the men that were working. Magna jerked her arm away from him and hissed as she bared her fangs.

"You may think you are the master of the castle, but I was the mistress of this castle long before you arrived," she sneered. "I will never take orders from you, here or in the bedchamber. This is my castle, and I will do as I please."

She turned her back on Jario and stormed off through the Grand Hall. Stopping by the door, she turned to look at Jario for a moment. She raised her arm and flicked her wrist giving Jario a firm push in his chest. Seeing him stumble, she gave him a wicked smile and vanished in a wisp of red smoke.

"I see you have a temperamental vampire on your hands," Gautier smirked, as he watched Jario regain his balance.

"Yes, she can be very difficult, but I do enjoy her company now and then," Jario replied, as he winked. "She can make an evening extremely enjoyable or quite excruciating. Anything that causes screaming heightens her pleasure and her madness. Do not worry, the screaming is deadened quite well in the stone walls of the dungeon."

"I have no need to entertain her company," Gautier replied. "Kayleigh is my true mate and all that I will ever need. We were separated unnecessarily, and I am glad to have her back in my arms. I will cherish her for all eternity and kill anyone who attempts to separate us again."

Jario shook his head in understanding and then replied, "Shall we make our way to inspect the repaired bedchambers? With the spell you offered to increase the workers strength, we are making good progress and near completion. Your help is greatly appreciated."

Nodding, Gautier followed Jario out of the Grand Hall and replied, "I owe you a great debt for ending the binding spell and giving me back Kayleigh. I will gladly assist you to right the injustice done to you."

"I am honored to have you by my side," Jario said, as he began to think of the things he would do to Thomas and how he would take Lady Lara for his own.

* * *

After leaving the castle in a very angry state, Magna walked among the trees spotting some of Jario's workers washing in the small stream that ran through the forest. Sadly, they were too thin to be strong soldiers, but they were men, after all, and had everything they needed to fulfill her needs.

She moved further upstream, but close enough that she could be seen among the trees. Pulling the laces from under her breasts, she loosened and removed her corset and dropped it to the ground. Untying the cords from her skirt, she pushed it, along with her under slip, down over her hips and stepped from the thick pile of fabric. Looking to see if the men were still bathing, she kicked off her slippers and stepped naked into the water. She deliberately splashed as she stepped to draw the attention of the men downstream. Turning her back to them, she bent over at the waist and cupped her hands to gather the cool water. Carefully bringing her hands up to her chest, she let the water spill from her hands and run down over her breasts. Continuing to pretend to bathe in the stream, she listened to the men as they heard her splashing and began to move toward her.

"What do we have here?" asked the tall man with the beard. "We found ourselves one of those mermaids everyone talks about, but this one is without her tail."

"Are you needing a bit of help with your bath, little lady?" asked the short bald headed man. "I could wash your pretty backside for you or anything else that needs a washing."

"Oh! Oh, I thought I was alone," replied Magna, trying to sound surprised and embarrassed as she covered herself with her hands. "You have found me naked and in the middle of my bath. If you were gentlemen, you would let me finish my bath while you turn around."

"She is calling us gentlemen," whistled the man through the space in his teeth. "I can wash you right nice since I am the only gentlemen here. We is all naked too, so don't be worrying your pretty head about it."

"You can be looking at our naked bodies all you want," said the bearded man. "Fair is fair. We all like naked women, right gentlemen?"

The other men nodded agreeing with the bearded man.

Continuing to cover herself with her hands, she motioned with her head hoping they would turn around. Surprisingly, she watched as they all turned around and gave her a moment of privacy. Stepping from the water, she picked up her slip holding it above her breasts to cover the front of her body. Walking around to face the grinning men, she gave them a wicked smile and held out her arm dangling her under slip between her fingers.

"Who among you knows how to dry the water from a woman?" Magna asked, as she put her other hand on her hip. "My body is wet, and I will need your help."

All of the men spoke at once as they anxiously offered their desire to help her. She tore her slip into three pieces and handed each man a small remnant of cloth. The men eagerly grabbed the cloth and started to wipe the water from her body. Overlooking her arms, legs and back, the remainder of her body was meticulously dried and then dried again.

Feeling refreshed, she walked about swaying her hips and looking over her shoulder. Stepping toward the tall man with the beard, she looked directly into his eyes as she said, with compulsion, "You will stand here, without speaking, until I release you from this spot."

The other men laughed at the strange way she was speaking to their friend.

Moving to stand in front of the man with the missing tooth she smiled and ran her finger down his chest. Drawing his attention, she looked into his eyes and uttered softly using her compulsion, "You will stand here, without speaking, until I release you from this spot."

The bald man stood looking at the men that appeared to be frozen in place. Not understanding what she was doing to them, his nerves got the better of him and he shivered slightly as he mumbled something she didn't understand.

"Looks like you are the lucky man," Magna said, as she reached for the man's hand. "We are going to have some fun."

She looked into his eyes and used her gift of compulsion as she spoke, "you will pleasure me, and when you are through, I will do things to you that will bring on my madness. You will not scream. You will not try to run away. You will feel everything I do to you."

Magna spread her skirt upon the ground and sat down upon the layers of fabric as she beckoned the bald man to kneel before her. Try as he may, he only succeeded in his own release. Pushing him off her body onto his back, she let her claws extend. Displaying her claws for him to see, she brought down one sharp claw at the base of his neck and raked it across his chest. She could see the pain upon his face and regretted silencing his screams. Seeing the blood run from the gashes, the hunger slammed into her throat. She took his wrist and bit down letting the dark red liquid wash over her tongue and down her throat. After covering most of his body with gashes and bite marks, she straddled his hips and dug her fangs deep into his neck taking his blood until she felt his heart begin to fade. Standing and walking back to the two men, she took their wrists and drank until they were both slumped upon the ground.

"You can thank Jario for my behavior," she said, as she walked back and forth in front of their unconscious bodies. "He is not my master. He cannot control me. I am the Mistress of Black Thistle Castle. It is my castle, and it will always be my castle."

Not wanting a scolding from Jario if he should hear of her display of frustration, she wiped their minds of everything that happened between them. She tore her wrist with her fangs and dripped her blood into their mouths. As they began to heal, the evidence of her brutality began to fade.

Feeling angry about the men wanting to take advantage of her, she left one last command for them. "Once I have vanished, you will wake and only remember that you fell asleep after pleasuring each other until you were exhausted."

She attempted to smile, but tears began to fill her eyes. Wiping the tears and the blood from her face with the back of her hand, she gathered her clothes and vanished to the security of her dungeon. Leaving no evidence behind, the men woke to the memory and embarrassment of their intimate escapade with one another and the fading wisp of red smoke.

Chapter 6

Lara heard the bedchamber door open and smiled, as Thomas made his way to her side. He bent down and kissed her forehead and sat down to begin pulling off his boots.

"I need to discuss something with you," Lara said, as she watched his smile turn to a worried frown. "I have not heard from Jario. There is no need to worry. I promised I would tell you if he enters my mind again. I need to tell you what I have discovered about Gavenia."

"What of Gavenia? Is she not improving?" Thomas asked, as he reached for Lara's hand.

"She is improving, but has not spoken with anyone since waking. Flora tells me she is eating simple food and will respond to questions requiring a nod or shake of her head. Niobe brought her to the exercise pen to visit me and see the horses this evening. I can tell that she enjoys watching them very much, and she even touched Mona without any fear," replied Lara, as she lovingly touched Thomas' outstretched hand.

"It is good news that Gavenia is up and about," said Thomas, as the look of concern left his face. "Is this what you wanted to discuss with me?"

"It is good news, but it is what happened when we were about to leave the pen that has me troubled. Gavenia heard birds fluttering in the trees and this seemed to cause her to run towards them. I thought that to be a little strange, but she stumbled and then had great difficulty breathing. Flora had to use her healing gift to bring her breathing back within her control. When she stood, there were feathers scattered upon the ground," Lara said, as she pulled the white speckled feathers from her pocket and handed them to Thomas. "I have spoken to Woodward, and he tells me that these feathers are from a Peregrine hawk. I believe that Gavenia is a shifter and that she was trying to shift into her hawk form."

Thomas' brows lowered over his eyes with concern and he asked, "Does this bring any danger to Evergreen? What is a shifter? As you know, I have only recently become aware of vampires and witches. I am almost afraid to ask what other creatures are walking amongst us."

Lara smiled and lifted her hand to stroke Thomas' face. Entering his thoughts, she knew he was confused, but he was more worried about protecting his mate and their people than anything else.

"A shifter is a human immortal that can take the form of an animal. Taking the new form allows them to have the powers afforded them of that animal. If Gavenia is a hawk, she will be able to fly, hunt birds and bats, and possibly gain information for Evergreen while sitting unnoticed among the trees. I want Gavenia to visit with Meadow for confirmation of my suspicion," she replied.

"If Gavenia is a shifter, how do we help her?" Thomas asked. "If this is something that has happened since being held prisoner at Black Thistle Castle, she will need help understanding her new form. If she has always been a shifter, she can explain to us what she will need to make her more comfortable."

"I love how concerned you are for our people. It makes me love you more. I will arrange for Gavenia to visit with Meadow tomorrow evening," Lara said, as she stood and offered her hand to Thomas. "Enough talk of Evergreen and shifters."

"I know that look," Thomas said, as he stood and wrapped his arms around her waist feeling her face rest against his chest. "My eyes are tired and need rest. If I will be enjoying your lovely body this evening, I will need to let my vision fade so that I can fully enjoy you later."

"Flora has drawn us a steaming bath," Lara said, as she led him to the bathing chamber. "We can soak, and you can rest your vision until the water turns cold."

"I would enjoy a steaming tub with you, my sweet," he said, as he untied the tight laces of her dress and watched it fall exposing the creamy skin of her shoulders. "I will try to rest my vision, but it will be a struggle to deny my eyes the pleasure of your beauty."

Lara stretched up on her toes as she kissed his lips lightly while her fingers found the ties to his breeches. Untying the leather cords, she stepped back to pull the heavy fabric over his thighs and take full advantage of the view that he offered. He pulled his tunic over his head and dropped it to the floor. Scooping her up in his arms, Thomas carried her into the bathing chamber. He stepped into the tub, and they slowly sank into the steaming water.

"To have your body next to me is pure heaven," Thomas whispered, as he kissed behind her ear and moved his fingers slowly down her arms.

"I thought you needed to rest your vision," Lara replied, feeling his arousal against her back.

"Do my talents amaze you?" Thomas asked, as he ran his hand across her abdomen toward her amber curls. "I can easily kiss and caress my mate with my eyes closed. Should I show you what other talents I can perform with my eyes closed?"

"If we want this steaming water to stay in the tub, I suggest . . . you save your many amazing talents . . . for our bed," she stammered, as she felt the soft caresses of his fingers upon her skin.

"You do, do you?" Thomas chuckled, as he continued exploring her body. "I didn't know that resting my vision could be so satisfying."

* * *

Thomas sat on the edge of the bed and ran his hands through his hair. He stood and stretched his body thinking about the lovemaking they had enjoyed through the evening and on until the sun had started to dim. Pulling his vision, he gazed upon Lara's naked body tangled amongst the bed linens. Her long strawberry curls sprawled over her shoulders hiding where he had lovingly trailed kisses from her neck to the dimples in her lower back. He loved the heat that raced through his body whenever they touched, and he always longed for the next time she was safely wrapped in his arms.

"I feel you looking at me," Lara softly whispered, as she lifted her head to glance over her shoulder at Thomas. "Come hold me my dear for a little while longer. I'm not ready to leave this bed. I find I need more of your sweet kisses."

Thomas moved swiftly and sat upon the edge of the bed. His large hands pulled her hair to the side as he tenderly placed kisses upon her neck and shoulders. She always smelled of lemon and mint, and he loved how it lingered on his body after they made love. He turned her gently and looked into her blue eyes. Those eyes had captured him long ago and had finally made him whole. He reached to pull her toward him when suddenly the sound of someone running could be heard coming from down the hallway. As the running ceased, heavy pounding upon the bedchamber door ended his thoughts of taking Lara one more time.

"My Lord, please come quickly. Tate has sent me. You are needed within the Council Chamber. There is trouble in the village," gasped the young Page.

"Can I not enjoy my mate without some village disturbance?" shouted Thomas, as he stood beside the bed clenching his hands into fists. "Give me a moment."

He dressed quickly and stormed towards the bedchamber door. Yanking the heavy wooden door open, he saw the Page trembling in the doorway.

"My Lord, I am sorry to disturb you, but Tate insists that it is urgent," responded the Page, as he backed away from the door giving Thomas room to leave his chamber.

Looking over his shoulder he gave his mate a regretful look that he would have to leave her. Lara sat up holding the bed linens to cover her naked body and nodded letting him know that she understood.

"We will continue this later," she said, as she smiled and blew him a kiss.

Hesitating for a moment, Thomas reluctantly turned and followed the Page through the stone hallways and into the Great Hall. The flickering light from the rustic torches bounced across the stone walls. It displayed a large dark shadow drifting upon the wall as Thomas strode through the room toward the Council Chamber.

As he reached the door, he could hear the voices of Tate, his brother and faithful right hand, and Preston, his trusted Commander of the Army. Thomas pushed the heavy carved door open and joined his council gathered around the large table. As he nodded to Tate and Preston, he took in the serious faces of his council members.

"What has Jario done now?" shouted Thomas, as he pulled out his chair and sat down motioning everyone else to do the same.

"My Lord, it appears that the repairs of Black Thistle Castle have been completed and many of the men have already started to return to their families. It has taken much less time than expected to rebuild the castle," said Tate.

"This warranted me being pulled from the arms of my mate?" barked Thomas.

"Our inquiries have given us some disturbing news," Tate replied. "A warlock by the name of Gautier, has taken up residence in the castle. There are tales of a great hatred between Gautier and the old witch, Velsa."

"If Jario and Velsa are not enough to worry about, we now must worry about a warlock too," snapped Thomas. "What other news have you brought me?"

"I have spent many an evening at the tavern to prevent the trouble that seemed to come along with all of the new arrivals," added Elda.

"Many men spoke of feeling stronger than they ever had before. Other men spoke of seeing men lifting large stones with their bare hands. If this is true and not a drunken rumor, the men must have been spelled to be able to perform tasks without the use of ropes or horses."

"I have seen a white wolf wandering among the tents at night," responded Will. "Keeping a great distance so as not to be scented, I have watched the wolf run across the drawbridge into the courtyard of the castle. I thought it to be a dog at first, but it is clearly a wolf. Has Jario found a way to tame a wolf?"

"How many of the men are staying at the castle?" asked Thomas. "I fear that those that stay will become the makings of Jario's army."

"I have counted twenty men," replied Will. "They are moving their tents from the meadow into the courtyard. A new wall is being built around the castle, as well as, small stone cottages within the wall."

"It is clear that Jario is building an army, and it is just a matter of time before he attacks Evergreen," declared Thomas. "We all know his desire for Lady Lara. Now that he has become the master of Black Thistle Castle, he must be planning on the destruction of Evergreen. We must be able to defend Evergreen and find a way to defeat Jario. Preston, last we spoke you were to develop a plan to protect Evergreen."

"We have stationed men at the warning towers beyond the castle. This will give us an early warning if trouble should approach us. Each tower has a messenger hawk to provide communication between the towers and the castle," answered Preston.

"Have we enough weapons to defend us from the humans within the army?" asked Thomas, as he felt his vision slowly fade and leave his eyes.

"Yes, the weapons are readied, as well as, the horses and wagons," Preston replied. "We have also dug pits filled with sharp stakes lining the bottom. This should handle both humans and vampires."

"The Page that came for me spoke of trouble in the village," said Thomas, as he turned his head in the direction of Tate's scent. "What kind of trouble are they facing? Lady Lara will be distressed if her people are suffering."

"We believe that a new vampire has been attacking folks leaving the tavern late at night," replied Tate. "The bodies have been drained and bite marks made from fangs have been found on their necks and wrists. We believe the fangs are from a vampire and not from an animal like a wolf."

"Track this new vampire down. Lady Lara will decide if it can be saved or must be put down," ordered Thomas. "Elda, since you have been working the tavern, I will rely on you to capture this vampire. Do not go alone. Take someone with you."

"Stay behind after this meeting, and we will discuss a plan to capture this new vampire," Elda spoke directly to Oliver.

Hearing Oliver's typical grunt of agreement, Thomas asked, "Does anyone have anything else to offer? Questions? Are we clear on our duties?"

Hearing nothing more than their usual eagerness, Thomas stood and dismissed the council. Seeing that Thomas had lost his vision, Tate stepped around the table and took his arm

"I will see you back to Lady Lara," Tate said, as he pulled the chair from his legs and guided him out of the Council Chamber. "Are you losing your vision?"

"No, I was just getting ready to sleep when the Page knocked on our door demanding my presence," replied Thomas.

"You have all of eternity to enjoy Lady Lara," Tate chuckled. "Don't risk the gift of your vision by being foolish."

"It is not foolish for me to look upon my mate," Thomas replied sternly. "I do risk being able to protect her if my sight is gone, and I understand your warning. You will not understand how I feel until you are mated."

"I will always be here to help you, my brother," Tate replied, as he put Thomas' hand upon the door handle of their bedchamber. "I love you both and will give my life to protect you."

"I love you too, my brother," Thomas replied, grateful and happy that Tate had been returned to him.

"Now, go rest," said Tate. "Do you hear me? You need to rest."

Thomas nodded and pushed the door open. Stepping into the bedchamber, he heard Tate close the door. Making his way to the bed, he stripped off his clothes and crawled into bed wrapping his arms around Lara. Closing his eyes, he felt the comfort of her body, and the darkness of sleep quickly took him.

Chapter 7

A small group of men, twenty at Jario's count, stood in the courtyard. They made four straight lines and stood quietly waiting for Jario to speak. Each man had been given a dagger to hide within the leather lining of his boot and a sheathed dagger to wear upon his hip. These men were all that were left after the work at the castle had been completed. Each one had volunteered to stay and become a member of the Black Thistle Army. The effects of the strengthening spell had long worn off and what was left was a group of weak unskilled men.

As Jario paced back and forth in front of the men, disappointment was reflected upon his face. He had felt the need to give the men a choice to enlist or to return home, and to his dismay, most of the men made the choice to return to their families. He was not surprised, but there were many he had hoped would have taken his offer of joining his army.

"You have all volunteered to join the Black Thistle Army," Jario shouted, for all to hear. "In doing so, each one of you must swear allegiance to me as the Master of Black Thistle Castle and obey Buck, the Commander of the Army. You will each wear the mark of the army upon your chest. Once you have sworn your oath and accepted the mark, you will be trained and afforded the respect of your station. If anyone here has decided against joining the army, step from the line and leave now."

The men looked around to see if anyone would step forward and leave. Each man stood firm within the line and eagerly awaited Jario's direction.

"Very well. Buck, I leave them in your charge," Jario said, as Buck stepped forward.

"The mark you will receive bears a dagger that represents the protection you will provide to your master, the castle and its people. The sharp points that encircle the dagger represent the thistles that surround this castle. They are strong and draw blood from those that mean us harm. Once you complete your training, you will be strong and skilled in the ways of shedding the blood of our enemies," Buck proudly addressed the men. "Now repeat the oath after me."

> I willingly pledge my loyalty to Lord Jario and the Black Thistle Castle.
> I will accept orders without question and defend my brother with my life.
> I will give all I have and expect nothing in return.
> To fail is to receive my death.
> To prevail is to bring honor to Black Thistle Castle.

The men repeated the oath as Buck recited every line. Once complete, the men cheered and slapped each other on the back as Buck clapped his hands and shouted words of encouragement.

"Now, follow me to the side yard and receive your mark," he shouted.

The men cheered as they left their formation and followed Buck in a single file making their way to receive their mark. Standing next to a pit of smoldering coals, Magna waited anxiously for the men. She took hold of the iron rod and held it up allowing the men to view the glowing red mark that would leave a permanent scar upon their chest. Returning it to the coals, she watched the men cringe and took delight from the fear in their eyes.

"This will be painful, but show your strength and do not cry out when you receive your mark," Buck stated, loud enough for all to hear. "A generous meal will be afforded to all that take the mark without showing weakness. Who will be the first to take the mark?"

A brave man stepped from the line and made his way to the smoldering pit as Magna pulled the glowing rod from the coals. He closed his eyes and felt the rod press into his chest over his heart. The smell of burning flesh filled his nostrils, and he gritted his teeth keeping his suffering silent. He felt the sting of his raw flesh as the rod was pulled away. Magna inserted the rod back into the coals and waited for the next man to prepare for his mark.

One by one, Magna pressed the glowing rod against their chests hoping to hear them scream. To Magna's dismay, none of the men screamed or made a sound. Her only delight was the anguish displayed across their faces as she pressed the hot glowing rod into their flesh. Throwing the rod back into the pit of coals, she watched as the men followed Buck over to the out building that they would call home.

* * *

The long wooden table was piled high with meat, cheese, eggs, and vegetables. A roar was heard when cups of ale were placed next to each man's plate. A few of the men looked around in surprise. For some, this was more food than they had ever seen at a single meal. For others, it was more food than their family had consumed in a month.

Buck sat at the head of the table and raised his cup in the air as he loudly hailed, "To the men of the Black Thistle Army."

The men raised their cups and cheered. Downing the ale, they all slammed their cups on the table and several men reached for the pitchers that held more of the amber liquid. Hearing the door open, they all turned to see Lord Jario, followed by Gusty, enter the room. Immediately, the men stood at attention. Gusty pulled the chair back allowing Jario to take his place at the head of the table. Taking the seat next to Jario, Gusty poured ale into Jario's cup.

Looking about the table of men and raising his cup in the air, Jario spoke as he made eye contact with each of the men, "I have been told of your strength as you received the mark, and I am here to thank you for your pledge to this castle and to me."

The men all raised their cups to Jario and shouted, "To honor Black Thistle Castle. To honor Lord Jario."

"Your training will start tomorrow. It will begin with longswords. Gusty will be in charge of assigning each of you into groups. Work hard and you will become a skilled member of the army. An important assignment is ahead of you. The sooner you are trained, the sooner it can be completed and benefit our goals," Jario sternly said. "I will always demand the best from you, and you should demand the best from each other. I will leave you to your meal and your celebration."

Gusty stood and pulled Jario's chair back allowing him to stand and move from the table. Reaching the door, he pulled it open waiting for Jario to exit the room. Jario turned and gave the men a slight wave before he stepped through the doorway. Gusty followed behind him closing the door. Several of the men started to breathe deeply after hearing their leader offer his appreciation and his challenge. The silence lasted for only a moment, as a man sat down and stabbed a piece of meat and yelled, "Let's eat."

* * *

Gusty followed Jario to a room filled with empty shelves and a large table covered in parchments and maps. They were discolored with age, and dust covered stacks of leather bound books piled in the corners. Jario reached for a map that he had been studying earlier. He unrolled the heavy parchment and set a smooth stone on each corner to keep it from curling.

"I have marked the entries to Evergreen Castle and added the new outbuildings on this map," Jario said, as he pointed to several different items upon the map. "The warning towers are located around the castle in these locations marked with a circle. I know these well. I stood watch within the towers for many a night when I joined their army. The towers are large enough for two men only. There is always at least one vampire and never two humans."

"Are they more vulnerable during the daylight hours?" Gusty asked. "Our army could attack while the vampires are trying to stay within the shade."

"Several of the vampires have the gift of walking in daylight. Our humans would not have the strength to overtake them. I believe the cover of night would work to our advantage," Jario replied, as he searched for another map.

Finding the small discolored map, Jario carefully unfurled it and placed it upon the table over the other map. Gusty added small stones to the corners to secure it in place.

"I discovered this small map and dismissed it for the larger drawings, but I realize now what it displays," Jario said, as he pointed to several lines that were drawn stretching out beyond the castle. "If I am correct, these lines represent tunnels from Black Thistle beyond the meadow ending within the Evergreen Forest. If we can find these tunnels and they have not collapsed over the years, we could use them to hide our army. It would give us the ability to surprise our enemies."

"Tomorrow, in the light of day, I will assign a few men to start searching for the tunnels outside the castle. If the army used them, I do not believe that they would have made access from inside the castle," Gusty said, as he looked to see if Jario was in agreement.

"Good," Jario responded. "The sooner we find the tunnels the better. They would offer us a great advantage to attacking Evergreen."

Jario made his way to the door as Gusty started to remove the maps from the table.

"Leave them out," Jario said. "I may study them later."

"As you wish, My Lord," Gusty replied, and followed Jario out the door and then headed for the army quarters.

Walking through the hallways, Jario smiled, as he thought of the coming attack on Evergreen and the capture of Thomas. He would make him feel pain for taking Lady Lara from him. He would make him watch as he took her as his mate. Feeling aroused by the thoughts of having Lady Lara's naked body beneath him, he headed down the stone steps to the dungeon. He had not visited Magna since her tantrum and felt the need to feel her body pressed against his own.

Entering the dungeon, Jario looked about the dim space for Magna. He could smell her lingering scent and knew that she was close. She had taken advantage of the large space and had a private bedchamber built within the dungeon. Why she insisted in staying within the darkness, he did not know.

Making his way to the door of her bedchamber, he pushed the door open to find Magna sprawled naked across the deep burgundy bed linens. Her eyes were closed and her hands were moving over her body.

"I have come to apologize," Jario said, as he made his way into the chamber and closed the door.

Magna opened her eyes and turned her head to face him.

"When you are in my bedchamber, I am the Mistress of Black Thistle Castle and you will obey me," she barked, as she sat up and moved to the edge of the bed.

Jario removed his boots and dropped them on the stone floor. He stepped forward and stood between her legs as he removed his tunic. He watched as Magna extended her claws and gave her a smile of approval.

"Will you scream for me?" Magna asked, as she lightly drew her claws over his chest and then snapped the leather ties to his breeches.

"I will obey, My Lady," he responded, as he let his breeches fall to the floor.

Magna smiled, as she rested her claws upon his hips and pressed her lips to the trickle of blood that ran down his chest. She could feel his arousal against her breasts and knew he had readied himself for the pain she was about to offer. Leaning back to look into his eyes, she raked her claws across his hips and heard the first of his screams.

Chapter 8

Niobe sat cross legged behind Gavenia at the foot of her cot. She ran a comb through Gavenia's newly washed hair trying to be careful of the patches that were recently healed but still looked pink and tender. She sang a song she had learned as a child, and Gavenia made a soft humming sound as she twisted a green ribbon between her fingers. Flora watched the women as she gathered the wet bathing sheets and soiled linens taken earlier from Gavenia's cot.

"Niobe, I need to take these linens to be washed," Flora said, as she peered over the bundle within her arms. "I expect a visit from Lady Lara and Meadow this evening. Please stay close to Gavenia. I believe that she may be afraid of Meadow."

"I will not leave her side," answered Niobe. "Gavenia likes me near."

Niobe heard Flora leave with her bundle and continued to comb Gavenia's hair. Singing again as she worked, Gavenia hummed and swayed her body to the melody. Satisfied she had Gavenia's hair dry enough, she held out her hand for the ribbon. Gavenia held the ribbon with her fingers and dropped it into Niobe's open hand. Pulling Gavenia's hair back from her face, Niobe started to braid her hair as she carefully wove the green ribbon through the long red strands. When she was finished, she moved the braid over Gavenia's shoulder letting her see her handiwork. Gavenia smiled and ran her finger over the ribbon within her red braid.

"It is beautiful," Tate said, as he leaned against the open doorway. "May I come in for a visit? I will not stay long."

Gavenia looked over her shoulder and nodded. She uncrossed her legs and turned to put them on the floor. Niobe placed her shawl across Gavenia's lap to cover her bare legs as Tate walked into the room and sat on the cot facing her. She noticed he held one hand behind his back, and she looked at him with curiosity in her eyes as she leaned to see what he had hidden. He smiled and pulled a handful of flowers tied with a ribbon from his back. Seeing her smile, he attempted to hand them to her. Gavenia hesitated for a moment and then carefully took the flowers making sure not to touch his fingers. She brought the flowers to her nose and inhaled the sweet fragrance. Moving them toward Niobe's face, she wanted her to share in the wonderful scent.

"I thought they might bring a smile to your face, and I see that they did," he said, as he watched her green eyes brighten. "Niobe has done fine work. The ribbon in your hair matches your eyes."

Gavenia blushed and moved her hand to cover the bald patches where her hair had not yet grown back. The look of sadness filled her eyes. She lowered her chin and looked down at the floor.

"Do not worry, sweet Gavenia. It will grow back, and you will be even more beautiful," Tate said, trying to comfort her.

Hearing the sound of skirts rustling outside the door, Tate looked up to see Lady Lara and Meadow coming through the doorway. Niobe started to help Gavenia stand, but Lady Lara put her hand upon her shoulder and shook her head.

"My Lady," Tate said, as he stood and brought his fist over his chest. "I see you are here to visit with Gavenia; I will make my leave."

Seeing Gavenia look up at him, he smiled and said, "I will visit you, again soon."

She brought the flowers back to her face and nodded. The need to touch her kept him from leaving, but he forced himself to move toward the doorway. Turning, he bid Lady Lara and Meadow good evening and headed back to the exercise room.

Gavenia's eyes drifted back to her latest visitors and watched Meadow's hair move wildly above her head. Curious, she pointed to the mysterious strands of hair and lifted her shoulders in puzzlement.

"This is Meadow," Lara softly said. "She is a friend to everyone at the castle, and she is here to help you. I told her of your trouble to breathe when you visited the horses, and she thinks she knows the cause. Will you allow Meadow to touch your arm? It will help her find a remedy that will provide you relief."

Gavenia pulled back and leaned toward Niobe looking to her for reassurance. Niobe grasped her hand and smiled. As she nodded her head, she softly whispered, "I will be here with you. Meadow will not hurt you."

Lara could sense that Meadow had released a mild feeling of relaxation and watched as Gavenia calmed and slowly nodded her approval. Meadow moved to kneel before Gavenia and lightly placed her hand upon Gavenia's arm. Meadow closed her eyes and searched for Gavenia's spirit. It wildly moved about her body trying to avoid Meadow's touch. As she calmed the anxious spirit, she saw flashes of blue sky and a beautiful white hawk soaring above the castle. It made several circles within the sky above the towers of the castle and then gracefully landed near the edge of the forest. Slowly the hawk transformed into a slim woman with red hair and green eyes. She stepped into the forest and retrieved a bundle of clothes from behind a tree. Dressing quickly, she stepped from the forest and ran for the castle.

Meadow patted Gavenia's arm and then pulled her hand away as she whispered, "Thank you for trusting me."

Meadow stood and sat upon the cot next to Lady Lara. Taking her hand, she gently pushed the images of the white hawk to her mind to allow her to see what she had seen. Lara watched the beautiful images of the white hawk that confirmed her suspicions. Satisfied with what she had seen, she looked over at Gavenia.

"Will you walk with us outside?" asked Lara. "It is a beautiful night, and I think you will enjoy the fresh air and the many stars that we can see in the night's sky."

Gavenia nodded and pulled the shawl from her lap. She stood slipping her feet into the blue velvet slippers that were a gift from Lady Lara. Pulling the shawl around her shoulders, she took Niobe's hand as she followed Lady Lara and Meadow through the hallways to the courtyard.

* * *

Gavenia slowly walked about the courtyard stopping to smell the fragrance of each flower that bloomed in the moonlight. Lifting her face to the star filled heavens, she watched a bright star shoot across the sky and followed its trail until it was gone. Seeing Niobe pick a bloom and place it in the water of the fountain, Gavenia did the same. They stood and watched the blooms float among the swirls of the water.

Meadow chanted under her breath, and the air around Gavenia took on a slight shimmer. Gavenia let go of Niobe's hand and stepped out of her slippers. Dropping her shawl, she scurried to a patch of green set among several smooth stones and laughed as she wiggled her toes in the clover. With a faint sigh, her sleeping gown fell to the ground. She seemed to disappear from view and then the sound of flapping wings were suddenly heard as a beautiful white hawk took to the sky. She soared above the castle and appeared to dance on the cool night breeze. Everyone watched in amazement as she sped through the sky testing the strength of her wings.

"Will she come back to us?" Niobe asked Meadow, as tears filled her eyes. "She won't leave us, will she?"

"Yes she will come back to us," Meadow replied. "She has found her hidden spirit, and she is enjoying the new feeling. When she tires, she will return to us."

Seeing her circle lower and lower, Niobe clasped her hands waiting for her to land. Hearing the sound of her wings overhead, they all watched as she landed upon the gown that had fallen from her shoulders. Her talons caught on the gauzy fabric, and her sharp hooked beak pulled at the fabric trying to release it. Seeing the same shimmer within the air around Gavenia, she suddenly stood naked before them.

Thrilled with what she had seen, Niobe ran to her clapping her hands. "You were wonderful," she said, as she wrapped the shawl around her body to cover her nakedness. "I could not believe my eyes."

"It was grand, was it not?" Gavenia said, as she smiled and wrapped her arms around Niobe. "Did you see me? I was flying above the castle. I cannot believe it; I was actually flying."

"We all saw you; it was truly wonderful," Lara said, as she picked up Gavenia's slippers and her sleeping gown.

"Gavenia, you have found your voice and your hair has grown back," Niobe shouted, as she ran her hand over the tresses that hung loosely outside of the tight braid. Niobe ran her hand over Gavenia's arm as she found it smooth and free from any healing marks. "Look! Look at your arms. Your marks are gone."

"She has healed herself in the transition from hawk to her human form," Meadow stated, as she took Lady Lara's hand. "Her new spirit was hidden and needed a little help to make itself known to her. She felt it outside at the pen, but since she was ill, she did not have the strength to allow the transition."

"Will I be able to change whenever I want?" Gavenia asked.

"Yes, you should be able to call your hawk whenever you want or need her," Meadow replied. "You will need to learn about the dangers in the sky and on the ground before you fly alone. An arrow that seeks the heart of a hawk will surely bring the life of the hawk and the human to an end."

Gavenia listened closely to Meadow, and then she asked, "Who will help teach me the ways of my hawk? I am sure I will have much to learn."

"We can discuss your hawk tomorrow," Lara said, as she handed Gavenia her gown and watched her pull it over her head. "Let's get you back inside the castle. You can sleep in the Healing Room tonight, but tomorrow we will find each of you a new bedchamber and some proper clothing. It is nice to see you well, Gavenia."

"Thank you, My Lady. Thank you, Meadow," Gavenia sniffled, as tears of joy ran down her face. "I hope to repay your kindness one day."

* * *

Holding her skirt up high over her boots for the third night in a row, Elda grumbled as she walked next to Oliver on their way to the tavern. Her legs itched from the coarse stockings she had tethered above her knees with cords of thin leather, and the plump tops of her exposed breasts kept drawing Oliver's unwanted eyes. She stopped, for what seemed like the hundredth time, to untangle her under slip from thorns, rocks, or whatever form of nature insisted on grabbing at her clothes as they walked.

"You made the plan," Oliver chuckled. "Do not blame me for your womanly awkwardness. Besides, where would you find a woman's frock that would fit the size of this manly body?" He stopped for a moment to display his large frame to her with his arms stretched out wide as he continued his teasing.

Elda glared at him as the hem of her skirt caught yanking her backwards one more time.

Finally reaching the tavern, it was decided that Oliver would crouch within the bushes that lined the dirt road next to the tavern. He would keep watch while Elda stood under the lantern as if she were waiting for a paying customer. They hoped to draw the rogue vampire out into the open and capture him.

"Give it your best come-hither look, Elda," Oliver whispered under his breath, knowing that she could hear him. "Let him get a look at your womanly charms." He could see Elda stomp her foot in anger and laughed at her attempt to look seductive. "Do not scare him away, my little muffin."

The door to the tavern opened, and two men staggered out onto the dirt road. Seeing Elda standing alone under the lantern, they elbowed each other and snickered as they approached her.

"What's a pretty little lady like you doing out here alone?" the taller man said, trying to keep his balance as he thrust his hips at her. "Are you needing some company?"

Elda ignored them and moved away from the glow of the lantern's light.

"If you be looking for a man," the man slurred, as he stumbled and fell to the ground. "Sorry, me thinks me had one too many ales."

He managed to get to his hands and knees before he fell again. Standing, he leaned against his friend as he beckoned Elda toward him.

Oliver stymied his need to laugh, but knew they had to get rid of these men if they hoped to draw out the vampire. He rushed up behind them and grabbed their necks pressing hard enough to make them slump unconscious to the ground. Picking them up, he hid them behind the wooden barrels on the side of the tavern and dashed back to the bushes.

"You can thank me later," Oliver whispered, as he watched Elda roll her eyes.

The wind swirled as it blew in from the harbor. The fresh scent of salt lingered on the breeze, and she relaxed as she leaned against the wooden post that held the glowing lantern. Elda could hear the crickets as they chirped back and forth to each other. The occasional outburst of shouting could be heard coming from the tavern, followed by the echo of Lulu's tray hitting some poor soul over the head.

Thinking they had wasted their time hoping for the vampire to appear before them, Elda was about to give up and head back to the castle when she heard the sound of someone running. It was faint, but the sound was heading their way.

"Do you hear that?" Oliver asked, as he saw Elda nod her head. "Someone is coming fast, too fast for a human."

"I am ready for him," Elda replied. Lifting her skirt to expose her leg from her hip to her ankle, she waited for the vampire to approach.

Bursting through the bushes onto the dirt road, Elda saw the man she had encountered in the tavern and had later given a broken wrist. He stood before her with a wild look in his red eyes. Recognizing her, he grinned as he let his fangs descend.

"We meet again," Cummings hollered. "You shamed me, wench. You shamed me in front of the men in the tavern. Power is in me now."

"What are you planning on doing with all that power?" Elda asked, as she readied herself for an attack.

"Me plans to be taking what you owe me," he shouted. "Plans to be taking your body and your blood before me rips your throat out."

"Strong words for a new vampire," Elda calmly stated, while watching for any indication of an attack.

"Ready and strong," he said, as he sprinted toward her, screaming with rage.

Before he realized her hand moved, he saw a dagger pressing into his stomach. Pushing her away, he freed the dagger from his body. He watched her slam into the wooden post and the lantern swing violently from its hook over her head. Oliver raced from his hiding place and pulled Cummings' arms behind his back. He struggled to free himself as Elda slipped on leather gloves and pulled a pair of shackles from her bag. Clasping them around his wrists, Cummings cursed as he staggered from the burning pain of the spelled shackles against his flesh.

Elda pulled the hem of her skirt up from between her legs and tucked it into the leather band about her waist. Taking Cummings by the arm, she turned him to face her.

"You didn't take the time to notice that I have powers too," she sneered, as she looked to see if Oliver was ready. "Your crimes have earned you a cell in the Evergreen dungeon. Your fate will rest in the hands of Lady Lara. I would make my peace, if I were you. From what I have seen of you, she will be condemning you to a final death."

Oliver picked Cummings up and threw him over his shoulder. Elda took off running as she led the way back to Evergreen. She was eager to get back to the comfort of her breeches and out of the awkward abundance of heavy fabric that consumed her body.

* * *

After listening to Woodward and Tolin discuss the dangers that lurked in the forest, Gavenia followed Tolin to an open stall in the corner of the stable. He had draped a horse blanket up to give her privacy when she removed her clothing, as well as, enough space to allow her to maneuver in her hawk form. She watched as Tolin left the stall to meet with Woodward and Meadow in the clearing.

Kicking off her slippers, she felt the fresh straw beneath her feet and inhaled its wonderful scent. Stepping behind the blanket, she untied the laces of her dress and let it fall upon the soft straw. Feeling the cool air upon her bare arms, she pushed the ribbons of her under slip off her shoulders and watched it land upon her dress. Stepping out of the ring of fabric, she concentrated on transitioning into her hawk and nothing happened. Closing her eyes, she tried again without result.

I can do this, she thought, as she took a deep breath and tried to focus.

Closing her eyes again, she thought of her hawk and the wonderful feeling she had as she flew in the cool night air. Her body began to shiver and tingle causing her to drop to her knees. Keeping her focus, she visualized her hawk's beautiful white feathers and her sharp talons. Holding her breath, the spirit of her hawk took over and replaced her human body with a beautiful white hawk. Hopping from the stall, she took to the air and flew over the heads of her friends.

49

"Watch how fast she can fly," said Woodward, as he lifted his face to the sky to take in the beauty of her white wings. "She is probably faster than any other bird in the sky."

Gavenia's hawk circled the castle spotting Lady Lara's courtyard. She dove down and landed upon the edge of the fountain dipping her beak into the water. Taking flight again, she continued to fly small circles until she was above the castle and made her way to the forest. Soaring above the tops of the trees, she flew as fast as she could to the edge of the forest and back to the clearing ready to make another loop. Noticing Woodward waving his arms, she headed back over the trio's heads hearing his voice calling for her to return. Wanting to ignore him, she forced her hawk to obey and return to the stable. Running through its open door, Gavenia headed straight for Meadow and threw her arms around her neck.

"She is magnificent," Gavenia cried. "I drank from Lady Lara's fountain and flew to the edge of the forest. I even saw the meadow full of wildflowers. She loves to fly."

Out of the corner of her eye, Gavenia saw movement coming from around the corner of the stable. Turning, she saw Tate walking toward the castle doorway.

"Tate, I can fly," shouted Gavenia. "Did you see me? I can fly."

Stopping as he heard her shouting, Tate saw the group huddled in the clearing.

"What?" Tate shouted, as he ran to meet Gavenia.

He looked surprised to see her and even more surprised to hear her speaking. The patches of her scalp that had been healing were now covered with hair.

"You are well?" he asked, as he gazed over her long red tresses.

"Something amazing has happened to me," Gavenia smiled and clasped her hands together. "I have the spirit of a hawk within me, and she has healed me. I can change into a beautiful white hawk and fly. It is the most wonderful thing that has ever happened to me." Looking at Meadow, she begged, "Please, may I show him?"

Tate stood stunned, watching Gavenia's green eyes sparkle with happiness. Woodward looked at Meadow, and she nodded her head. Seeing Meadow nod, Gavenia ran back to the stable.

"How did this happen?" Tate asked, as he looked at Meadow for an explanation.

"We only just discovered the possibility yesterday," she replied. "Last evening she transitioned into her hawk. When she transitioned back to her human form, she was able to heal herself."

Hearing the flap of her wings, Tate looked up and watched Gavenia soar in the sky. Diving down low, she flew close enough to make Tate duck his head. Smiling, he watched the beautiful white hawk circle the clearing and return through the stable door.

"We want to speak to her about watching Black Thistle Castle," Woodward said. "She has good control over her flight, but she still needs to learn to spot danger to keep herself safe."

"I can work with her," Tate offered. "She needs to learn the sound of an arrow and how to avoid them."

"Speak with Thomas and Preston," Meadow said. "We met with them, and they know of her ability. Preston is already working on a plan to use her new skill."

Gavenia ran from the stable smiling and joined the group. Tate took her hand and covered it with his other hand feeling the heat race through his arm. Her eyes told him that she felt it too.

"You were amazing, Gavenia," Tate said. "I am so happy you are well and you have found your hawk spirit."

Letting go of her hand, the heat left his body, and he saw Gavenia look at her hand with curiosity. Seeing Meadow turn toward the castle and Gavenia follow, he said his goodbyes to Woodward and Tolin and followed the women back to the castle.

"Thank you Tolin. Thank you Woodward," Gavenia shouted, over her shoulder. "You helped make it a glorious day."

Chapter 9

The clashing of swords could be heard coming from the army quad. The quad, as it was called, sat in the middle of four army barracks which sheltered the army's activities from anyone sent to spy on their strength or numbers.

Gusty walked toward the men quickly spotting those that showed promise. Impressed, he was relieved to see there were a few men out of the group that actually had skills. Looking over the rest of the men, he needed to select two or three that he would order to start searching for the hidden tunnel entrances. Noticing a man that could hardly hold his sword over his head and two men bent over heaving their morning meal, Gusty knew his choice was clear. These men would never meet the demands of the army and would not be missed if they were lost in a collapse of one of the tunnels.

"Anthony, Charlie, Drake," Gusty shouted, gaining their attention. "Stow your swords and come with me."

Waiting for the trio of men to meet him in the corner of the quad, he watched as they slowly placed their swords in the hollows of the wooden stand.

"Run! I will not wait all day," he barked. "You are in the army, act like it."

The men turned and ran toward Gusty gasping for breath and fearing the reason for the summons.

"I have a special assignment for the three of you. It has been determined that there might be tunnels that lead away from the castle to the Evergreen Forest. It is your job to find the secret entries to the tunnels. If you find one, you are to enter it and make your way as far as the tunnel leads. If an escape is visible at the end, carefully make your way to the outside. It is important that you are seen by no one. You will need to describe where the exit is located and make note of your surroundings using landmarks. Landmarks that will allow for the entrance to be found quickly if danger is near. Make your way back to the castle through the tunnel and mark the entrance. We believe there are five tunnels based on the markings from an old map," explained Gusty. "Do you have questions?"

"What if the tunnel is blocked?" asked Drake.

"For now, come back and clearly mark the tunnel entrance and continue to search for additional tunnels," Gusty replied. "Lord Jario wants this completed as quickly as possible. His need for these tunnels is urgent."

"Are we to search together or alone?" asked Charlie, as he looked at the other men hoping he would not be alone. He feared the dark of tight places.

"Stay together as you search," Gusty replied. "If one of you should be injured, you will need someone to seek help. Any other questions?"

Seeing the men shaking their heads, he handed each a skin of water, a leather pouch containing a small flint, a bundle of candles, and a torch soaked in animal fat. The men took time to attach the skins and pouches to the leather bindings about their waists. Each man, with a torch in hand, followed Gusty to the main courtyard to start the search.

Taking in the view of the courtyard, the huge space seemed to overwhelm the men. They looked at each other and walked toward the inner wall. Heads down and three abreast, the men began to walk examining the ground for any sign of a hidden entrance. Back and forth they stomped their feet trying to hear any change in the surface under their boots. They occasionally stopped to move large stones or pick up a piece of charred wood over grown with clover.

Hours later feeling the assignment was next to impossible, Drake tripped over something that was completely covered by clover. On hands and knees the men pulled the clover from the ground to find four small wooden planks secured to one another with metal bands. Pulling the dagger from his boot, Drake wedged the blade between the wooden planks and the ground, but his prying motion was met by resistance. Fearing he would break his blade, he sent Anthony to get an iron rod to give him more leverage. Moments later, Anthony returned with the rod, and Gusty running closely behind him.

"Sir, we believe we found one," Drake shouted, as he reached for the rod and shoved it into the small space made by his blade.

Charlie picked up a rock and placed it securely under the rod on the ground providing the leverage he needed to pry up the planks. Seeing Drake struggle without result, Gusty gripped the rod below Drake's hands to help. The combined strength forced the planks to split with a loud crack and fall into the dark space below.

"Who wants to go first?" Gusty asked, looking at the men's faces.

"I will," volunteered Anthony. "I am the smallest and lightest. Take my hands and lower me down. I don't want to jump and kill myself."

Anthony sat with his legs dangling over the side of the opening. Gusty laid down on his stomach and took Anthony's wrists and felt him grab his own. He watched him scoot off the edge of the opening and drop into the dark space.

"I can't feel the bottom," Anthony said. "Don't drop me."

Charlie and Drake each grabbed a leg and allowed Gusty to stretch further into the opening, as he bent at the waist. Anthony reached for the bottom with the toes of his boots and felt nothing.

"I still cannot feel the bottom," Anthony said, feeling the sweat running from his forehead stinging his eyes.

"Drake, let go of me and light your torch. Drop it in the hole," Gusty ordered, fearing he would be dropped in the hole on top of Anthony.

"Wait," Drake said. "I see a tall ladder leaning against the top of the stone wall. Let's pull him out and try the ladder."

Drake helped Charlie pull Gusty back and retrieve Anthony from the darkness. Hauling the ladder over to the opening, the men maneuvered the ladder down into the dark hole, hoping to feel it hit the bottom. With only one rung of the ladder left above the opening, the men felt the resistance of the wooden ladder when it made contact with the bottom of the hole. Taking only a moment to slap Drake on the back for his idea, Anthony made his way down the ladder, and they heard him shout when he reached the bottom.

A slight glow from Anthony's torch could be seen by the other two men as they made their way safely down the rungs of the ladder. Looking up, they saw Gusty holding a rope and heard him holler just before it fell from his hand. Drake picked it up and through it over his shoulder. Examining the tunnel ahead of them, they looked at each other fearing what they would find. It felt damp and reeked of mold making the men want to gag. They knew that this could easily be their death trap, if the tunnel should collapse and bury them alive. Bending at the waist, the men entered the tunnel and began their search for the other end.

* * *

Rocks and dirt tumbled down from the narrow walls as the trio walked cautiously through another tunnel. Fearing they would meet with another collapse, the men were careful to watch where they stepped. The torch Drake carried provided some light within the darkness, but it was not enough to keep from tripping on the roots that twisted within the damp earth. Coming to another section of narrow tunnel, the men had to turn their backs against the dirt wall and carefully slide through one at a time. Feeling their backs brush against the crumbling wall, they could hear more dirt and rocks falling around their boots. As the tunnel widened, the men loudly exhaled trying to make themselves feel less claustrophobic. After regaining their composure, they continued to make their way through the cramped space until Drake noticed what appeared to be a dead end.

"We have reached another dead end," Drake shouted, as he waved the torch about the tunnel trying to examine the earth before him. "It must be the end, it does not look like the other tunnel that collapsed. It is too solid to be a collapse."

"Look up for a wooden door," Charlie yelled, as he pointed to the mass of roots above them. "There might be a way to get out of here."

Drake moved the torch over his head as far as he could reach watching the flame highlight the tangled roots above his head, but it gave no view of a trapdoor. Bringing the torch down, he exhaled the breath he had been holding hoping for a way to leave the musty tunnel. Anthony fidgeted from one foot to another and then turned thinking it was time to give up and head back to the entrance.

"Anthony," Charlie said, as he nudged him in the side. "Get down on your hands and knees next to me and let Drake stand on us. Maybe, he can find a trapdoor."

Giving him a disgusted look, he bent down next to Charlie and felt the pressure of Drake's boots upon his back making him groan. Drake shoved the torch into the nest of tightly woven roots trying to find wooden planks. He grasped the roots with his other hand and pulled watching them snap and fall away. Slowly, light began to seep through the gaps made from removing the roots, and it revealed a rusted strap of metal.

"I see something," Drake shouted, with excitement as he stepped down and pulled his dagger from his boot. "Charlie, hold the torch for me. Sorry Anthony, I need to stand on your back again to reach the door."

Once again on his hands and knees, Anthony mumbled his complaints as Drake stepped upon his back. Drake began to cut away the roots that hindered his view and access to the wooden planks. Slowly, he hacked at the roots and dropped the dry pieces to the floor of the tunnel revealing more and more of the door above them. After much effort and constant complaining from Anthony, the planks were finally free of the roots that had encased the planks. Drake pushed his dagger through a gap in the planks without much resistance. Pulling his blade back, he shoved it along the edge of the door several times to loosen the earth. When he thought he had given the door enough freedom to move, he tucked his dagger into the leather around his waist and firmly pushed the planks with both hands. Drake closed his eyes and felt the dirt fall from the edges of the door. One by one the planks pushed through to the ground above, filling the tunnel with the forest's filtered light.

"You did it," shouted Charlie, as he watched Drake jump up from Anthony's back resting his abdomen against the edge of the opening.

Carefully raising his leg to the surface, Drake crawled out of the tunnel and cautiously looked about for any sign of danger. Seeing none, he squatted down and signaled the men to ready their way clear of the tunnel. Looking about the forest, he saw a group of boulders and secured his rope around them and lowered it down to the men. Each man made his way out of the tunnel into the fresh air and sat brushing the dirt from their hair and face. As they gulped large breaths of air trying to rid themselves of the musty dampness they had been breathing, they tried to straighten their strained backs. Taking a moment to rest, they pulled the skins full of water from their waists and drank deeply.

Wiping the back of his hand across his mouth, Drake reminded the others, "We need to remember what we see around the entrance of the tunnel. Buck will want a description of the door's location."

"I see three boulders," said Anthony, as he pointed to where Drake had tied the rope.

"There is a group of new evergreens within six large paces," Charlie added.

Nothing out of the ordinary seemed to be within eyesight of the tunnel. There wasn't a stream or downed log that would easily offer a clue to the tunnel's entrance.

"We have to leave markers around the area to help us find the tunnel," Drake said, as he showed the men how to stack small rocks one on top of each other. "Before we leave the markers, let's do some exploring, but be quiet in case someone from the Evergreen Army is in the forest."

The men walked through the trees looking for anything that might help them in finding the tunnel, if on horseback or on foot. They walked a good fifty paces from the tunnel and then stacked stones against a small boulder covered in moss. Turning left and trying to keep the tunnel entrance to their left, they proceeded another fifty paces. Leaving a pile of stones in the hollow of a tree, they felt satisfied that it would be a good marker. Continuing to pace a boundary around the entrance, they left stones at a tree stump, at the corner of a cluster of ferns the size of a bed cot, and at the base of a tree that had three broken arrows embedded in the trunk. Pleased with their markings, they headed back to find the boulder where they had first left the stones. Finding it, they knew they had completed their assignment.

Making their way back to the tunnel entrance, they talked about the dreaded journey back through the narrow damp space. They all wanted to head back to the castle on foot above ground but did not have weapons for their protection. Standing over the entrance, Charlie looked about the ground for something to disguise the tunnel entrance. They gathered branches and leaves and covered the wooden planks of the door ready to make their way back down the rope into the tunnel. After Charlie and Anthony descended, Drake untied the rope from the boulder and secured it over his shoulder. Sitting at the entrance edge, he moved the covered planks closer to the opening. Turning over onto his stomach, he moved his legs down the tunnel and felt Charlie grab them. Taking hold of the planks, he carefully pulled it over the opening as Charlie helped lower him into the tunnel. Lighting the torch, the three men made their way back through the tunnel heading for Black Thistle Castle to report their findings.

Chapter 10

The Evergreen dungeon was occupied by a single vampire, and he had been screaming since being locked in his cell. Elda stood outside the dungeon door listening to his vulgar outbursts of the things he wanted to do to her once he was free. Little did he know that his freedom was in question and possibly his existence? She stood patiently waiting for the arrival of Lady Lara. She would examine the thoughts of the vampire and make the final decision about his fate.

Thomas escorted Lara through the hallway to the dungeon. After hearing the report from Elda and Oliver, he wanted to be present when the vampire was questioned. He wanted to know if Jario was behind the vampire attacks within the village. Hearing their footsteps, Elda opened the door leading to the dungeon cells and stood at attention holding the door as they entered.

Standing in front of the cell, Lady Lara made eye contact with the vampire. She could see the hatred in his eyes and knew he was filled with madness.

"My name is Lara, and I am Mistress of the Evergreen Castle," Lara calmly addressed the vampire within the cell. "What is your name?"

"Cummings is me name. You cannot keep me here," he shouted, as he reached through the bars trying to grab her. "Me done have powerful friends that will see this castle in ruins."

"Who are your friends?" Lara asked, as she slowly entered his thoughts.

"He be called Buck. He be the commander," he replied, waiting for some expression of fear to be seen upon her face. Instead, he shook his head as he felt a slight pressure behind his eyes as Lara made her way through his thoughts. "He done give me his blood to heal me broken wrist. Your little wench caused me pain and shamed me in the tavern." Lifting his wrist to let her see the wrist that she had broken, he snarled at Elda. "He done give me a choice to be a vampire. Me done took it and wanted me revenge on the little wench." He let go of the cell bars and pointed toward Elda. "The little wench that stands by the door. Me demands you give the little wench to me. Me wants to hear her squeal when I pound her from behind." Cummings laughed and jutted his hips in Elda's direction. Wiping the spit from his chin, he continued to rant. "You be seeing Buck will rescue me real soon. You be seeing Buck is stronger and can surely kill you. He be snapping your bones."

Cummings gripped the bars and threw his head back as he laughed. He began to bang his head against the bars as he mumbled to himself. Closing his eyes, he tried to push the pressure from his mind. Lara patiently waited for him to regain his focus.

"I see," she replied, as she continued to search his thoughts. "Does he allow you to kill the people of my village? If so, he is not my friend."

"Me have the free will to do as me pleases," he answered, as he spit upon the floor of his cell. "Now that me have power, me can do as me pleases."

"I am sorry that you were not given guidance when you were human or when you were turned," she stated, taking a step back and withdrawing from his mind. "I have discovered that you have killed men and raped young women for pleasure. This was done as a human. You continued these deeds as a vampire. I will not offer you the chance to escape the madness. I sentence you to a final death. I sentence you to a final death for the protection of my people."

"You cannot harm me," he laughed and blew kisses to Elda. "I know secrets."

"I know all of your secrets, your thoughts, and all your wicked deeds," she answered, with a disgusted tone. "I wish I had not seen them. They were vile."

Lady Lara turned and took Thomas' arm. He led her through the open door and out into the hallway. Cummings' vulgar rantings could still be heard until Elda followed them out into the hallway and closed the door.

"Elda, come with us to the Command Center," Lara said, with concern upon her face. "He has been spelled by Meadow and cannot leave his cell. Preston will see to his final death."

* * *

Entering the Command Center, Lara signaled Preston to join them. Watching Preston move toward them, Thomas felt the slight tremble of Lara's body and pulled her hand to his mouth, kissing her palm. Smiling up at Thomas, she brushed his face with her other hand before she turned toward Preston.

"I am ordering the final death of the vampire, Cummings. I have read his thoughts and know of his crimes as a human and a vampire," she said, with sorrow in her voice. "I fear he is beyond saving."

"I will carry out your order, My Lady," Preston said, as he brought his fist over his heart. "It will be done justly and quickly."

"His thoughts held conversations he overhead between Jario and Gustavo. They are building an army and planning an invasion of Evergreen," Lara said. "We must be vigilant."

"The warning towers have been manned and patrols are run daily through the forest, the village and the docks." Preston responded. "The army is prepared. We will be ready to protect Evergreen and its people."

"There is something else," Lara said. "A warlock named Gautier resides at Black Thistle Castle. He is very powerful and dabbles in black magic. He is mated to a white wolf, Kayleigh."

"Have you had an encounter with this warlock or his mate?" Thomas asked, searching Lara's eyes for any clue of harm they may have caused her. "Do you fear him?"

"I was very young during the War of the Witches, but my father told me stories of a warlock that fell in love with a white wolf," she said. "Velsa secretly loved Gautier and hated him for taking the wolf as his mate. She banished him and his mate with a binding spell. The spell must have been broken. Velsa would not have broken the spell, and Jario does not know black magic. The spell must have broken by someone unknowingly. If it was broken by Jario, Gautier would feel indebted to him and obliged to do his bidding."

"Is the wolf a danger?" Elda asked. "Does she have any special powers?"

"It is not known if the wolf has powers," Lara replied. "We must be on guard and prepared to defend ourselves if we should encounter either Gautier or the wolf. I warn you to be careful around the wolf. A wolf bite is deadly to a vampire."

Hearing the side door open, everyone turned to see Tate and Gavenia enter the Command Center followed by Will and Oliver. Gavenia had exchanged her feminine attire provided by Lady Lara for the breeches and tunics worn by Elda when she was practicing the ways of her hawk. It had made disrobing before transitioning into her hawk much easier, especially if she was among the prickly plants of the forest. Happy to see Lady Lara, Gavenia smiled and bowed slightly as she greeted her.

"How is our little hawk?" Lara asked, as she brushed the stray hairs from Gavenia's face.

"She is wonderful," Gavenia replied. "I learn more and more about her every day. I believe that she is learning about me too."

"We have begun shooting arrows at her," Tate laughed, seeing the concerned expression on Lady Lara's face. "She can now maneuver away from any arrow shot from a crossbow. Her speed is breathtaking."

"Is she ready and willing to serve Evergreen," asked Lara, as she looked from Tate to Gavenia. "Is she ready to enter the Black Thistle Forest?"

"I am, My Lady," replied Gavenia. "It would be an honor to service you."

"Very good," responded Lara. "Preston, I leave it to you to discuss any plans that would require Gavenia's hawk."

"Yes, My Lady," responded Preston.

"I will leave you to your plans and a good evening. Thomas," Lara said, as she took his hand. "I need to speak with you in private."

Leading Thomas through the doorway, Thomas could hear Preston ordering everyone to the Council Chamber to discuss plans to spy on Jario and the Black Thistle Army. He felt the need to join the discussions, but Lara needed him more.

* * *

After closing the door, Thomas pulled his vision and watched Lara walk across the chamber to her chair. She sat down folding her hands in her lap and closed her eyes. He sensed how troubled she felt and wanted to give her comfort.

"I can tell by the look on your face that the need to speak to me is not about how much I love you," he said, smiling as he walked towards her. Kneeling down in front of her, he took her hands in his and gently kissed her palms. "Tell me what is troubling you and how I can help you." Remembering her previous invasion by Jario he asked, "Has Jario entered you mind again?"

"No," she replied. "I promised you I would tell you if he did."

"Then, what has you so worried?" Thomas asked. "You can tell me anything."

"I heard things in the vampire, Cummings, thoughts that scared me," she said, as her eyes filled with moisture. "Thomas, I heard things about us. Horrible things. Jario still wants me as his mate. He wants to give you a final death to make me his. He is building his army to be able to attack Evergreen. I fear that Gautier will use his black magic to help him."

Thomas stood and pulled Lara up into his arms. He held her tightly against his chest and kissed the top of her head. Feeling her body tremble made him angry.

"He will never have you," Thomas said, as his hand lifted her chin so he could look into her eyes. "There are many here at Evergreen castle that will protect you. I promise you, I will do all I can to protect you even if it means my final death."

"I will not survive without you, my love," Lara whispered. "You are everything to me. There will be nothing for me if you are not in my life."

"You are safe here in Evergreen," Thomas whispered. "I am with you and love you above all others. We can be cautious and prepared for what may come, but do not let Jario have your thoughts. Do not let him win."

"I love you above all others," Lara replied, as she stood on her toes to softly kiss his lips. "You are such a comfort to me. Jario will not win. Take me away from these thoughts of Jario and death. Fill me with thoughts of our love."

Without hesitation, Thomas lifted Lara into his arms and carried her to their bed.

Chapter 11

Patrols were increased after the capture and execution of the vampire, Cummings. Gavenia had made several flights over the docks, the village, and the Evergreen Forest, but always with someone to track her. She sat in the stable mentally preparing for her first flight over Black Thistle Castle without Tate or Woodward close enough to track her. Fidgeting with the laces on her breeches, she went over the path in her mind to allow her hawk to understand her assignment. Gavenia could feel her hawk anxiously awaiting to be released.

Standing, she pulled her tunic over her head and untied her breeches letting them fall about her bare feet. Folding her clothes and placing them on the wooden stool, she pushed the stall door feeling the cool breeze upon her skin. She stood with her arms relaxed and waited for her hawk to come forward. Dropping to the soft straw scattered about the stall, her hawk quickly appeared flapping her wings. Hopping from the stall, she took flight and circled the stable waiting for Tate to follow her.

Tate sat upon the back of Twiggs, a cinnamon stallion, as he watched the hawk leave the stable and circle over his head. Seeing her make one last circle, he gave Twiggs a nudge with the heels of his boots and galloped across the pasture toward the Evergreen Forest. He would follow the hawk to the far edge of the forest, and from there, he would watch Gavenia until she was beyond his view. Once she was finished with her observation, he would then follow her back to the stable.

She could see everything. The view from the air above the trees was beautiful. It was beautiful until she reached the edge of the forest and could see Black Thistle Castle off in the distance. The meadow separated the Evergreen Forest from Black Thistle Castle and it was very clear where the meadow ended. The lush green of the meadow vanished and was replaced by gray earth covered with black thorns of poisonous thistles. The black stone walls that protected the castle were dull and intimidating.

Clearing the meadow, Gavenia prepared to land on the near corner of the outer wall. Tate had told her about a protection spell, and she needed to know if it would stop her from flying over the castle. Swooping down and landing on the decorative ironwork, she relieved herself before hopping onto the wall. Feeling no sensation or resistance, she took to the air and headed for the stonework above the turret. So far, nothing prevented her from flying within the wall of the castle.

Sitting far above the grounds of the courtyard, she noted the holes that held partially exposed ladders. A few people walked about the courtyard and they were dressed in working apparel found among farmers. She could see the makings of a few partially built stone cottages and men constructing a thatched roof.

Taking to the air again, she flew over the top of the castle and landed at the top of the highest tower. Below her, she could see four buildings surrounding an area full of men in small groups wielding their swords. She counted fifteen men fighting in the center and two men observing. One man was covered in tattoos and the other man had dark skin. Taking to the sky, she flew about hoping to see the wolf. Not seeing anything else of interest, she headed back to the meadow. Swooping low to make it easy for Tate to see her, she saw him turn Twiggs and head for the thick forest.

Flying just above the tops of the trees, she could see small birds heading for cover. It tempted her to leave her course, but she kept going forward until she saw three men walking within the forest. They were all dressed the same and seemed to be searching the area. Circling back around, she flew down among the branches of the trees. The men were walking among the trees, but did not appear to be hunting. They did not have crossbows or simple bows over their shoulders. Not recognizing them as members of Evergreen, she flew back to find Tate. Seeing him below, she swooped down squawking to draw his attention. He stopped, seeing her low among the branches.

"What is wrong?" Tate asked. "Is there danger? If so, move in the direction you wish me to go."

Gavenia flew away from the direction of the men. Tate slowly followed her through the trees. Moving a good distance out of their path, she stopped and did not move.

"Do you want me to wait?" Tate asked.

She flew up through the trees and back to where she had seen the men. They were gone. Flying back to Tate, she landed near him and squawked before she took to the sky heading back to Evergreen.

"I hope that means it is safe," he said. "We need to work on some way to communicate."

Arriving back at the stables, he waited for Gavenia to leave the stable before he took Twiggs back to his stall. Seeing Tolin coming from the pasture, Tate waited as he approached. Tolin took the reins and brushed his hand over the neck of Twiggs.

"I will take care of him for you," Tolin said, as he led Twiggs to the stable. "Gavenia is waiting for you at the other end of the stable."

"Thanks," Tate replied, as he raced to meet her.

Gavenia leaned against the stable wall smiling with her arms crossed.

"You are too slow," she said, laughing. "Come with me. I need to tell Preston what I have seen at the castle and in the forest."

Holding out her hand to Tate, he slipped his hand into hers, and they ran to the Command Center. Heat ran up his arm, and he noticed Gavenia looking at her hand.

I am holding her hand, he thought. She wanted me to hold her hand.

* * *

Jario heard a knock at his chamber door. Magna quickly opened the door to find Gautier standing in front of her.

"Come in," she said, as she ran her hand over his arm as he passed her. "Two are more fun than one."

Hearing deep growling, she turned to find the white wolf baring her teeth. Stepping aside, the wolf entered the chamber and made her way to Gautier's side.

"It is getting too crowded for me," Magna snarled. "Jario, please do not let her on your bed. I hate dog hair."

Magna pushed the door closed and vanished.

"Keep her away from Kayleigh," Gautier barked. "Kayleigh will not hesitate to bite her, and we both know the danger of a wolf bite to a vampire."

"Point made," Jario replied, as he untied his new floor length cape. Shall we get down to business?"

"You have asked for a spell to allow you to change your appearance or to change someone else's appearance," Gautier responded. "Is this correct?"

"Yes, this is my desire," replied Jario.

"I can perform the spell," Gautier said, as he stepped forward and placed his hand on Jario's shoulder. "You will only be able to appear as another man. If you change the appearance of someone else, they will stay as if they were still a man or woman. You can only change their features. Does this meet with your desire?"

"Yes," Jario replied. "This will do nicely."

"Stand very still," Gautier ordered. "This will hurt during the spell and for a good time after the spell is done. Kayleigh my sweet, move away from us."

The wolf moved to the other side of the bed away from Jario and Gautier and curled up on the floor. Gautier placed his other hand on Jario's shoulder and closed his eyes and began to speak in a strange tongue.

The moment Gautier began to speak the spell, darkness took the sight of Jario's eyes and his skin burned from Gautier's frozen touch. He heard two words that he did not recognize and lost all hearing. He felt pain and then Gautier carry him to his bed. The pain was worse than anything he had ever felt. It continued through the night and never let him sleep. In the early morning, the pain began to ease and his sight returned. He sat up in bed and looked at his hands. They were covered in blisters. Panicked, he pulled his tunic from his body and found his chest covered with the same blisters.

"What have you done to me?" Jario screamed.

Gusty heard Jario screaming and ran down the hallway to his door. Not bothering to knock, he opened the door and found a man standing naked in the middle of his chamber covered in blisters.

"Lord Jario?" Gusty shouted, as he moved closer to the man. "Is that you?"

"Yes, it is me," screamed Jario. "I need Gautier. Hurry, I must be nearing my final death. He must have done something wrong."

Gusty ran from the room and headed toward Gautier's bedchamber. He pounded on the door and stood waiting for Gautier to answer. Gautier made his way to the door and opened it wide revealing the wolf standing near the bed snarling.

"Lord Jario needs your help," Gusty said, trying to control his voice. "He is covered in blisters and feeling great pain."

"I will come to him shortly," Gautier replied, as he closed the door in Gusty's face.

Gusty ran back to Jario's chamber to find him on the floor face down. Jario made no sound and did not move. Gusty knelt down next to Jario and touched the back of his head causing Jario to scream.

Gusty kept looking over his shoulder for Gautier but he wasn't there. It seemed like hours had passed before he entered the chamber. Gautier stood over Jario and spoke, "Stand, walk to your bed, rest in your bed until the pain is gone."

Obeying Gautier, Jario stood and returned to his bed.

"That is all you will do for him?" Gusty asked. "You tell him to go to bed. Did you not see him covered in blisters?"

"I saw the blisters," Gautier replied. "He asked for this spell. I told him it would be painful, and the pain would last for some time. When it is complete, the pain will be gone. The blisters will heal but they may leave scars. He will have the ability to hide them with the spell I gave him. Leave him. There is nothing you can do for him."

Gautier turned and left the chamber leaving Gusty standing confused. He walked to the bed and saw that Jario appeared to be sleeping. Sighing deeply, he struggled over leaving Jario alone but did as Gautier requested and left Jario alone in the bedchamber.

* * *

Climbing up the ladder from the damp musty tunnel, each man inhaled a deep breath of fresh air as they reached the surface. Glad to have returned to the castle without the tunnel collapsing on them, they laughed as they rubbed the dirt from their hair. Buck saw the men standing around the ladder and ran to meet them.

"We found the end of the tunnel," Drake yelled. "It went all the way to the forest."

"This is good," Buck barked. "Lord Jario will be pleased. Did you make note of the area around the tunnel?"

"Yes," Drake replied. "We marked five points around the tunnel. They are between fifty and one hundred paces from the tunnel entrance. We concealed the planks over the tunnel with branches to hide it."

"Your job is not complete," Buck responded. "It is important to know how long it takes to walk the tunnel and return. I need you to do this, again."

"You want us to go back down there?" Anthony asked Buck.

"Yes," Buck shouted. "Do you not understand an order? If this is too difficult for you? I can use you for target practice. That is an easy assignment."

"No, No," Anthony replied, running his hands over his face. "I can walk the tunnel for you."

"Good answer," Buck replied. "I will give you a chance to eat and sleep tonight, but I need you to walk the tunnel so I can time you."

Buck left the men standing in the courtyard. He wanted to find Gusty and Jario. He needed to tell them the news.

Exhausted, they watched Buck walk toward the castle door. The men hung their heads as they all thought about the tunnel. They all dreaded returning to the musty darkness. Drake kicked a rock and headed for the barracks. Anthony and Charlie followed closely behind. They were all ready for a bath and a good meal.

Chapter 12

After hearing about the men in the forest, Preston ordered Oliver, Will and Baxter to patrol the area as soon as possible for an extended period. If the men Gavenia spotted from the air were from Black Thistle Castle, they needed to be stopped. If they were from the village, they needed to be warned of the trouble that might find them in the forest.

Baxter readied his pack for the extended patrol. Throwing his pack over his shoulder he followed Will and Oliver out of the Command Center. Tate stood holding the reins of their horses and Gavenia's hawk circled the pasture ready to show them where she had seen the men. Mounting their horses, the men looked at one another with determination upon their faces. Nudging Twiggs, Tate turned toward the forest as the others followed.

It wasn't long before the men were deep within the forest and setting up camp. Seeing the horses were securely hidden, Tate bid the men good luck and continued on toward the Black Thistle Castle with Gavenia's hawk. Watching Tate follow the hawk, Baxter wished he could find someone to share his life. He loved the army, but he needed more. He needed a woman to share his bed and his life.

Gathering his thoughts back to the forest, he started making circles around the area where Gavenia had seen the men. Oliver and Will had gone deeper into the forest to search for any signs of hunter's traps or Jario's new army. He examined the forest floor for tracks made from army boots or the soft smooth leather soles of the hunters that frequented the forest. He could see that many animals had been through the area recently foraging for food. There were no signs of the remains of fires for cooking or blood from a wounded animal. The area was clean and basically undisturbed. The only signs that humans had been through the area were a couple of piles of small stones. The hunters often marked the areas that were found to be good for hunting with stacks of small stones. These stones could have easily been from them, however, it would be worth watching if Jario's army had decided on this location for a specific reason.

Seeing the pink and orange glow of the coming sunset, Oliver and Will made their way back to find Baxter and make preparations for the coming darkness. Baxter would not have the eyesight afforded vampires and would need their help. Arriving back at the camp, Will ran to help Baxter cover the canvas lean-tos with branches to disguise them.

"Oliver caught you a rabbit," Will said, as Oliver raised his arm to display a rabbit grasped in his hand. "Make a fire and I'll skin it for you."

"Thanks," Baxter grinned at Will and slapped him on the shoulder. "You two always look out for me."

"Gavenia told us that the men she saw on the grounds were all out in full sun," Oliver said, as he leaned his crossbow against the base of a tree. "That means they are probably human and have not been turned yet."

"Do you think he will have them turned?" Baxter asked, as he picked up the stones from the base of the tree he had seen earlier and started to make a circle for a fire pit.

"It seems unlikely," Oliver replied. "He would have a group of out of control vampires on his hands. Cummings was definitely out of control, and they would be too. New vampires would become rogue without containing them in cells. They would need to be spelled to comply or have the madness driven from them. Jario has not given this much thought."

Seeing the flames in the small circle of stones, Will handed the skewered rabbit over to Baxter to place above the fire. The smell of the rabbit cooking made Baxter's mouth water.

"Do you miss eating rabbit?" Baxter asked, as he wiped his mouth with the back of his hand.

"No," Oliver replied, laughing. "I can still eat rabbit. I just prefer the rabbit's blood."

Baxter grabbed his throat and gagged after hearing Oliver's comment. He watched Will laugh and try to mimic him too. Oliver quickly stood and started to move toward Baxter. Grabbing him before he could even stand, Oliver turned Baxter's head and lowered his mouth to his throat. Baxter and Will could hardly control their laughter.

"You are great, my friend," shouted Baxter, as he held his sides from the pain caused by his laughter. "If I had to be drained, I would pick you to do it."

"Your rabbit is burning," yelled Will, as he grabbed it off the fire and threw it at Baxter.

Suddenly, the sound of crunching leaves and snapping branches stilled the men. Oliver looked at Will and slowly pulled his crossbow from the tree. Will shook his head and pursed his lips in anger. They had not been paying attention to their surroundings. Carefully pulling his dagger from his boot, Baxter stood ready for an attack. They all watched as a plump raccoon lumbered into their camp site and slowly wandered on out through the trees. The men sighed deeply with a great sense of relief reflected on all of their faces, and they knew that they had been lucky. They had let down their guard and could have paid dearly for it.

Returning to the seriousness of their task, Oliver stood glaring into the forest while Will readied the camp for the night. Baxter sat quietly finishing his burnt rabbit and getting himself ready, mentally, for defending his friends if required.

"I will take the first watch," announced Oliver, as he looked at Baxter and then Will. "Finish up your meal, feed the horses and get some rest. We have to stay alert tomorrow."

* * *

Tate watched from the edge of the forest as the white hawk flew toward Black Thistle Castle. He wanted her to try and perch by an open window in hopes of discovering where the bedchambers of Jario and Gautier were located. She had decided to try and find Jario's chamber, first, in hopes of hearing him talk about his plans. Soaring above the castle, she looked for an open window. Assuming he would be in the upper floors of the castle, she spotted a small balcony with an open door. She cautiously landed upon its stone ledge. She could hear movement within the room and then painful screaming.

Was someone being murdered, she thought?

Hearing no calls for help, she waited fearing someone was dying. Listening for a threatening sound, she heard a door open, and a man with a deep voice ordered someone to bed. She heard footsteps and the crumple of bed linens. Two men spoke to each other before one of the men left the room. Waiting, she finally heard the sound of the door closing.

Curious about the cause of the screaming, she flew into the chamber landing on the back of a chair that sat next to a large bed. Sprawled naked upon the bed linens was a man covered in swollen oozing blisters.

Hearing the sound of her talons upon the chair, Jario's eyelids began to twitch. With a raspy groan, he slowly opened his eyes and looked directly at her.

"Have you come to take my spirit to the underworld," Jario asked, trying not to move any part of his body. "I was very foolish when I asked for the spell from Gautier. I find that I am ready to die my final death to escape this pain."

His eyes closed, and he moaned from the pain before he slipped back into the darkness. She watched him fall into deep sleep. Seeing enough, she flew from the chamber and headed back to find Tate.

* * *

Gusty stood in front of Jario's chamber door afraid to enter. He had seen his master covered in blisters the night before and hoped he had survived. Holding his breath, he opened the door to find Jario wrapped in his bed linens standing by the bed.

Hearing the door, Jario turned around to face Gusty and let the bed linens fall to the floor. Seeing a look of concern upon his face, Jario stepped forward.

"I have survived the spell," Jario said, as he turned around with his arms outstretched. "A white hawk came to me in my dreams and took away the death that tried to drag me to the underworld."

"Are you still in pain, My Lord," asked Gusty, as his eyes drifted over the remains of the blisters and the numerous red scabs. "Is there anything that I can do for you?"

"Draw me a bath," Jario replied. "I must wash the remains of these blisters from my body." Jario held out his hands and looked at the scabs that now covered his flesh. "Before you go, I want to try something and have you watch me."

Gusty stepped toward Jario and stood before him wondering what else Jario wanted him to see.

"Make my hair long and the color of wheat," Jario ordered.

Gusty stood with his mouth open as he watched Jario's hair begin to shimmer and grow until it hung beyond his shoulders. The golden color of wheat moved slowly from the top of his head to the ends of his new long locks.

"How did you do that?" Gusty asked, as he walked around Jario examining the long hair that now hung from Jario's head. He slowly brought his hand up and touched the golden strands to make sure it was real.

"I have been given the power through a spell," he replied. "This may be of great use to me. I can also change you."

Gusty stepped back, put up his hands, and shook his head as he spoke, "I am happy with the way I look, My Lord. There is no need to change me."

"Not to worry," Jario replied. "I will not force you to change. Draw my bath for me. I must ponder my new power."

Gusty headed for the chamber to draw his bath. Looking back over his shoulder at Jario, he felt cold slither up his back and knew he had to be careful. Jario was changing. He wasn't sure he was prepared to follow him.

Chapter 13

Drake and Charlie made their way to the courtyard. They had not seen Anthony since yesterday evening's meal. His cot had not been slept in and none of his belongings were missing. Everyone knew that he was not cut out for the army and was basically lazy. He had eyes for women and a thirst for too much ale.

"Where is Anthony?" Buck asked, as he looked over Drake's shoulder to see if he was just lagging behind.

"We do not know," answered Drake. "He was not in his cot this morning."

"I will take care of him when I find him," Buck snarled, as he took hold of the top of the ladder. "Do you have all the gear you need?"

"Yes," replied Charlie, as he dropped the torches down the hole. "Drake, I have the ropes. I also brought my bow. We didn't have any weapons last time."

"Good idea," Drake said, as he checked his pocket for the flint. "I would hate to run into trouble without a way to protect ourselves."

The men made their way down the ladder. Lighting the torch, they looked up at Buck and gave him a wave. Moving quickly, the men carefully walked through the tunnel. Without Anthony, the pace was much faster, and before they knew it, they were at the tunnel's end. Charlie knelt down for Drake to stand on his back. Drake reached up and pushed on the planks moving them to the side. Jumping up to lean his chest against the mouth of the tunnel, Drake pulled himself up out of the hole. Looking around to make sure there was no danger, he dropped the rope down for Charlie feeling his weight as he grabbed it. Pulling him up, they covered the entrance and moved out to check the markers.

"We can do it faster if we both check for the markers," Charlie said, hoping to get back faster.

"Sounds good to me," Drake replied. "Meet you back here when you are done."

They left in opposite directions and moved quickly keeping their eyes open for anyone from the Evergreen Army. Drake had found the first two markers but also found that a small fire had been used overnight. Careful to stay under cover of the surrounding bushes, he headed back to the tunnel. He bent down to prepare to uncover the planks when he heard footsteps. Looking up, he saw a member of the Evergreen Army with his bow drawn.

"Stand up slowly," Baxter ordered. "Do not reach for a weapon. I am a master with the bow, and you will be dead before you can draw one."

"I mean no harm," Drake replied, as he slowly stood and moved his empty hands away from his body. "I am hunting for our mid-day meal."

"That may be so, but I see the Black Thistle mark upon your chest," countered Baxter with a grin. "How many of you are in the forest?

"I am alone," replied Drake, as he took a deep breath trying to keep from shaking.

Baxter noticed his eyes scanning the forest. He knew that he was looking for someone.

"I doubt that," laughed Baxter. "It is not wise for a member of Jario's army to travel alone in the Evergreen Forest. Why would Jario send a member of his army out to hunt? Does the army fill the food stores?"

Drake was embarrassed. This man knew the army did not fill the food stores. Drake had not thought about what to say if he was caught close to the tunnel entrance.

"There are so few of us that we all have to share the work," replied Drake, fearing he had given away too much information.

"I see," Baxter said, as he circled around Drake looking for any weapons upon the ground. "He is having trouble finding men to support his wicked deeds."

As Drake nervously waited for Baxter to arrest him, he heard the faint whistle of an arrow and watched as Baxter fell to his knees. The shaft of the arrow was protruding from his chest and blood began to run from the corner of Baxter's mouth. Drake stood paralyzed watching him fall to his side. He feared the next arrow would be for him.

Charlie jumped from the bushes and yelled, "We need to get out of here. I have seen horses that belong to the Evergreen Army. They may be close."

Drake and Charlie ran to the tunnel and pulled back the planks.

Charlie jumped in first and looked up waiting for Drake to move his body over the entrance. Feeling his legs, he rested them on his shoulders and steadied Drake as he moved the planks over the tunnel. With the planks securely in place, he lowered Drake to the ground. Without a word, they began moving through the dark tunnel without taking the time to light the torch. Feeling light headed and hearing ringing in his ears, Drake stopped and bent over with his hands on his knees.

"I need to stop," Drake shouted to Charlie. "I am about to pass out."

Placing his hand against the dirt of the tunnel wall to steady himself, he felt lightheaded. He coughed and then gagged, as he vomited his morning meal.

Charlie ran back, taking his arm to keep him from falling. Hearing Drake slow his breathing, he helped him stand. Lighting the torch, he looked carefully at Drake.

"Are you able to move?" Charlie asked. "Can you walk?"

"Yes, my brother," replied Drake. "You saved me, and I owe you my life."

"Brothers have no debts," answered Charlie, as he took Drake's arm and moved him forward. "You are not my blood, but I consider you my brother. We need to keep moving. You will feel better once you are out of this tunnel and in the fresh air."

With Charlie's help, Drake stumbled through the tunnel. As the end of the tunnel began to brighten, the men relaxed and hurried to the ladder. Climbing up the ladder into the daylight, the men took in huge gulps of air. Pulling the skin from his belt, Drake drank the cool water it held until it was empty.

"You made good time," barked Buck. "Did you have any trouble?"

Charlie looked at Drake before he said, "Yes, I had to kill a member of the Evergreen Army."

* * *

Will and Oliver headed back to camp. There had been no sign of any men within this area of the forest. A few hunters' footprints following deer were the only signs left upon the floor of the forest. Feeling that it may have been an innocent group of men making their way through the trees, Oliver wanted to head back to the castle. Will stopped and held his arm in front of Oliver to keep him from moving.

"Do you smell that?" asked Will, as he inhaled the forest air. "It is fresh blood. It is human blood."

"Baxter," yelled Oliver, as he began to run toward the scent. "Heavens no, not Baxter."

Both men sped through the forest until they reached the place where Baxter lay crumpled upon the ground. They could see blood running from his mouth and nose. Bending down, Oliver carefully broke the arrow allowing him to roll Baxter over onto his back. His heart was still beating but it was faint. With each labored breath, blood gurgled in Baxter's throat and spilled from his mouth.

"We have to get him back to Evergreen," Oliver shouted. "He is almost dead."

Oliver scooped Baxter up in his arms, making blood gush from his mouth. Placing him back down on the ground, he struggled with what to do to help his closest friend.

Will tried to send his thoughts to Lady Lara. His forehead burned as he pushed his thoughts harder. Thinking he was not strong enough, he suddenly heard her voice.

"I hear you, Will," answered Lady Lara. "I will send Tate. He can bring him back quickly. If it is too late, do what you feel Baxter would want."

"Lady Lara is sending Tate," Will said, as he knelt down beside Baxter and took hold of his hand.

"I do not think he will last long enough for Tate to get here," Oliver replied, as he tried to wipe the blood from Baxter's face.

"Lady Lara said to do what Baxter would want," Will softly said, as he placed his other hand upon Oliver's arm. "What do we do?"

"We will wait as long as we can," replied Oliver. "We will wait, as long as we can, for Tate. I fear I do not have the strength to drain my dear friend."

"Oliver, he has been bleeding so much there cannot be much left," Will whispered. "Offer him your wrist. Try to heal him. Save him, please."

The sound of boots could be heard hitting the ground near the men. Looking up to see Tate running toward them, Will moved to let Tate see Baxter's limp body. Tate flinched at the sight of him. He put his fingers against his neck searching for the feel of a pulse. It was there, but it was faint and getting weaker.

"He is beyond the help of Flora's gift," Tate sadly said. "What is his request?"

"He asked me to turn him. When we became good friends, he asked me to turn him," replied Oliver. "He said he wanted me to do it."

"It may be too late, but try," Will said, struggling to keep control of his emotions. "He would do it for you, if he could."

Nodding, Oliver took his dagger and sliced the flesh of his wrist. As the blood began to run down his arm, Tate held Baxter's mouth open as

Oliver rested his wrist against Baxter's open mouth, letting the blood run over his tongue. Baxter made no attempt to draw from him and his eyes never opened. They all listened as his heart beat slowed and then beat for the last time. Their friend was gone. Tears fell from Oliver's eyes as he pulled his wrist from Baxter's mouth.

Tate silently stood with Baxter in his arms. Oliver and Will stood and touched Baxter's face before they headed for their horses to return to Evergreen. Tate kissed his friend's forehead and leapt from the forest to return him to Flora's loving hands for burial.

* * *

Lara and Thomas met Tate at the Healing Room. They watched him lay Baxter's body upon the linen draped cot. Tears fell from Lady Lara's eyes as she saw his lifeless body. Flora stepped forward placing her hand upon Baxter's chest and pulled the broken arrow from the wound. Dropping it into a woven basket upon the floor, she began to remove his tunic.

"I have much work to do," she said, looking at the saddened faces. "Leave me to prepare his body. He would not want you to see him like this."

Slowly they left the room leaving Flora alone. She removed his bloody tunic and dropped it into the basket she had placed by the cot. Pulling his leather boots from his feet, she set them down at the foot of the cot and untied the leather bindings of his breeches. Removing the bloody breeches, she placed them with his other bloody clothing. Heating the water within a large earthen bowl with her hands, she began to wipe the blood from his face and chest. Tenderly she worked, cleaning his body of every bit of blood.

Tate returned to the Healing Room, bringing an elaborate tunic and breeches. He flinched as his eyes saw the wound in Baxter's chest. He placed the clothing on the empty cot next to him and looked at Flora.

"Can you help me with his body," asked Flora. "I want to remove the soiled linen and replace it with a fresh one."

Tate bent down and picked up Baxter's limp body. After Flora replaced the linen, he laid him back down and watched as Flora dressed him in his burial uniform. Tate picked up his boots and began to clean them. He scrubbed until they were free of all the dirt and blood. Pulling them on Baxter's feet, he made sure the tops of the boots were even and everything was perfect. Looking over his friend's body, he was pleased with the way he was dressed.

"I will let Lady Lara and Lord Thomas know that Baxter is ready,"

Tate said, to Flora. "Thank you for taking good care of my friend."

"It was my honor, sir," replied Flora.

She watched Tate leave the room and turned to remove the basket of bloody clothes and linens from the room. Picking up the basket, she glanced back at Baxter.

Dropping the basket, she screamed, "Tate, come back!"

Hearing Flora scream, Tate ran for the Healing Room. When he entered the room, he froze as he looked at Baxter. Baxter was sitting up, and his red eyes stared back at him.

Chapter 14

Buck ran through the long hallway repeating over and over the words he would say to Lord Jario, "His men had found a tunnel that led to the Evergreen Forest, and they had maneuvered it twice without collapse. The entrance within the forest was bordered by several markers and it had not been found by the Evergreen Army. Charlie had created a problem by killing a member of the Evergreen Army. This could very easily start a war. A war that Black Thistle was unprepared to fight without an organized and skilled army."

Standing before his chamber door, Buck knocked waiting for the sound of Jario's voice to allow him entry. He could hear boots coming toward the door and was surprised when he saw Gusty standing within the chamber.

"Where is Lord Jario?" asked Buck, as he tried to peer through the open door. "I have important information that I must give directly to him."

"He is in the bathing chamber," Gusty replied, looking confused. "He is recovering from a spell that was performed by Gautier."

"A spell, was he injured?" asked Buck, with concern in his voice as he waited for Gusty to allow him into the chamber.

"I am not sure that injured is the right word to describe his condition," answered Gusty, as he backed from the doorway waiting for Buck to enter the chamber. "His skin is recovering from the effects of the spell. He was left covered with horrible blisters."

"Blisters!" Buck gasped, as he felt his chest heave from the thought.

"Yes blisters," replied Gusty, running his hand back and forth over his arm. Remembering the sight of Jario's face and hands made his eyes close as he tried to remove the vision from his mind. "What he can do now is really amazing, but it is also very frightening."

Buck backed away toward the door. He wasn't sure if he wanted to wait until Jario was finished with his bath. He could feel a thick layer of dread hanging in the air.

"I believe that I will wait to discuss things with Lord Jario," Buck said, as he reached for the door placing his hand upon the iron handle.

"What things?" Jario asked, as he walked from the bathing chamber holding a robe draped over his shoulders.

"Lord Jario," Buck said, as he stared at Jario's wet hair the color of wheat and the red marks upon his face. "What happened to you?"

"I changed my hair," he laughed, as he wrapped the long strands of golden hair around his fingers. "It is quite amazing, don't you think? Have you seen anything more wonderful than this? Can you imagine the possibilities?"

Buck watched Jario play with his strands of hair and then drop his robe to the stone floor. His body was in full view, displaying the residue left behind from the spell. The blisters were gone, but red marks covered every part of his body. Jario held his arms out for the men to see as he turned in a circle before them.

"Watch closely," Jario smirked, as he lowered his arms. "Make my red scars disappear."

Slowly, one by one, the red scars disappeared. As they did, his long hair began to change back to the short hair he had maintained. Delighted the scars were gone, he ran his hands over his body looking for approval from the two men that stood before him.

"It appears that the spell does not last as long as I had hoped," Jario complained, as he paced back and forth in front of the men. "I must speak to Gautier about my new power. Even if it lasts a short time, it can still be of use to me."

Remembering that Buck had wanted to speak to him, Jario bent down and picked up his robe. Throwing it over his shoulders, he walked over to the leather chair and sat down folding the robe in his lap.

"Buck," Jario beckoned him to come closer. "You had something to discuss with me?"

"Yes, Lord Jario," Buck replied, inhaling deeply. "We have found a tunnel that runs from the courtyard to Evergreen Forest. The men have maneuvered the tunnel twice without any collapse. However, we do have a problem. Charlie killed a member of the Evergreen Army."

Jario's bellowing laughter filled the chamber.

"Wonderful on all counts," replied Jario, clapping his hands and continuing to laugh. "I have wanted to kill a few of them for decades. Did anyone see him do it?"

"He appeared to be alone," replied Buck, watching Jario closely. "He only saw Drake before he died. He did not see who killed him, but he did know that Drake was part of the Black Thistle Army. He saw the brand on his chest."

"It does not matter," Jario smirked. "He is dead and cannot tell anyone who he saw in the forest. Very good. This is very good. Give the men my congratulations and bring a woman to their barracks tonight. They need to be entertained."

"Yes, My Lord," replied Buck, as he turned toward the door wanting to escape the thick evil feeling that hung in the air.

"Buck," barked Jario, as he stood letting his robe fall and waiting for him to face him. "Send word to Magna that I will see her tonight in her chamber."

"Yes, My Lord," replied Buck, as he left closing the door with a sigh of relief. Leaning up against the door, he closed his eyes and tried to calm his body. He could see the evil in Jario's eyes and knew terrible things were about to happen. The more power he obtained from Gautier, the more dangerous he would be to Evergreen and anyone that got in his way. He knew his time at Black Thistle Castle was coming to an end, either by Jario's hand or by running for his life.

* * *

Buck took the dungeon steps two at a time. He hated the dark dungeon and hated being alone with Magna, even more. He had let his desire for her give her the upper hand on a few occasions. He had always known she was dangerous, and he had firsthand knowledge of her viciousness. The worst being the night he had been strapped to the bed of spikes, and she had torn his chest to shreds. It had taken him days to heal. Seeing the pleasure she received from branding the men, made him cringe. Since coming to Black Thistle Castle, he had not had too many meetings with the female vampire, and he avoided her if he could. He knew he lost all control if he looked into her eyes. She had a way of making him forget all the evil things she had done to him. Taking the last step into the room full of cells, he heard moaning coming from the small cell at the end of the row.

"Magna, are you here?" Buck shouted, staying close to the stone steps. "Lord Jario has sent me. He wishes to see you tonight."

Not hearing any response, he stepped further into the dim light looking for what was making the pitiful sound. Reaching the last cell, he saw a man's body curled on his side with his ankles in shackles. Blood ran from wounds upon his legs, and his tunic was wet with fresh blood.

"Do not wake him," Magna whispered, startling Buck and making him jump. "He is sleeping. He needs his rest. I believe that I made things quite difficult for him."

"Who is it?" Buck asked, as he tried to back away toward the stone steps.

"He told me he is part of Jario's army," Magna replied, stepping closer to Buck. "I found that to be true. He wears the mark upon his chest."

"Why is he in the cell?" Buck asked, as he scanned the other cells. "Was he caught trying to run from Black Thistle Castle?"

"No, he came here willingly," replied Magna, as she smiled sensing Buck's fear. "He came to me to be turned. I had my fun with him and then granted his request. He will be waking soon, and Jario will need to train him if he wants to control him."

"Does Lord Jario know of this?" asked Buck, as he realized that Magna now stood between him and the steps.

"No, he does not," Magna said, as she shook her head and clinched her fists. Stepping closer to Buck, she could see fear emerging across his face. "This dungeon is mine. I am the mistress of this dungeon and all that enter it obey me. Why are you here? Are you back for more? The spikes were not enough for you? It has been a decade since we played together."

"I was sent by Lord Jario," Buck nervously replied, feeling the heat from her body skim over his face and fearing her claws. "He will come to your chamber tonight."

"Very well," Magna replied, as she backed away allowing Buck to move toward the stone steps. "I will prepare for his visit."

Buck moved quickly toward the steps. Hesitating, he turned to face Magna. Jario was changing, and he wanted to warn her.

"Is there something else?" Magna asked, tilting her head and rubbing her palm against her breast. "Would you like to stay with me until Jario arrives?"

"Mistress, be on guard," he whispered. "Lord Jario has received a spell from Gautier. A spell that left marks upon his body. He can change how he looks with one command. I fear this means great trouble for all of us."

Magna's eyes widened with concern as she stepped toward Buck and asked, "Have you seen him do this?"

"Yes," he replied, rubbing his hands over his bald head. "I have seen it with my own eyes. The air around him is thick and heavy with evil."

Turning toward the steps, he leapt forward to take the steps as quickly as he could. Magna watched him bolt from the dungeon. She had never seen fear in Buck's eyes. He was as wicked as they come, and she had watched him drink viciously from humans. For him to show fear meant, she should be very cautious. Hearing the new vampire moan, she smiled and turned to go back to her chamber. She needed to prepare herself for Jario's visit and consider the warning given by Buck.

* * *

Jario stood at the top of the steps and listened to the sound of someone moaning. He recognized the sound to be coming from a new male vampire. No orders had been given to turn any of the humans. This was Magna's doing, and she would be severely reprimanded for her actions.

Taking a few steps down toward the dungeon, his nostrils flared as he inhaled the scent of smoldering coals. Letting her scent surround him, thoughts of feeling her naked body under him encouraged his arousal. It was difficult for him to control his excitement and take the stone steps slowly. He wanted to race down the steps and command her a new appearance, but he took his time enjoying his secret.

Reaching the bottom of the steps, he saw that she had left the door to her chamber slightly open. The warm glow of the flickering candles within her room made dark shadows dance against the ragged stone walls. Pressing his hand upon the wooden door, he gently pushed it open to reveal the sight of her magnificent petite body. She sat at her dressing table pulling pearl capped pins from her hair. Each pin she pulled, released a long red strand of hair upon her bare creamy back. One by one, she released the pins allowing her hair to fall around her shoulders and upon the floor. She was beautiful, but not as beautiful as Lady Lara.

"You wanted to see me?" Magna asked, as she turned her head to look over her shoulder and up into his eyes. "Is this business or pleasure?"

"As your master, it is a visit of my choosing," he replied, smiling as he stepped toward her.

Placing his hand upon her shoulder, he ran his fingers down her arm and lifted her naked body towards him. Kissing the top of her head, he felt her arms wrap around him. Her claws began to extend from her fingers, and he felt them pierce his skin as the venom began to sting. Pulling her hair from her neck, he lightly kissed her shoulder. Letting his fangs descend, he nipped at her neck until beads of her blood settled on its surface. Flicking them quickly with his tongue, he threw back his head feeling heated desire race down his throat.

Bending his head back to her ear, he softly whispered, "I have something to show you. You will find it extremely entertaining, and it is only limited by your desires. I find it quite marvelous, and I believe that you will too."

Chapter 15

Word of Baxter's death moved quickly through Evergreen Castle and the surrounding villages. A heavy shadow of great mourning was felt by all, as well as, fear of an attack against the castle and their people. Evergreen had not lost a member of the army for decades and it had been over half a century since losing one by an attack.

Lady Lara ordered a ceremony with full honors for her faithful servant and charged Woodward with preparing the pyre. Baxter was loved by all and had been a bright burst of energy among the army. He had always put others before himself, and during his short life, he had given much honor to the army through his deeds and actions. He deserved this special honor.

The Council began to gather outside the door of the Council Chamber. As the members stepped back allowing Lady Lara and Thomas to enter, Lara could feel the pain that was displayed by their somber faces. She added it to the mounting pain she felt within her own chest. Lara watched as each member entered the chamber and stood behind their heavy wooden chair glancing at the empty chair where Baxter once sat. Lara stood at the head of the table with Thomas to her right. He placed his hand on the small of her back causing her to lean against him for comfort.

Tate had not arrived and they were all waiting for him to take his place before they started their discussions. Hearing light footsteps upon the stone floor, Lara looked toward the door expecting to see a message from Tate. Instead, Flora quickly entered the chamber.

"My Lady," Flora said, sounding anxious as she made a small curtsy and stepped toward Lady Lara. Looking about the room, she felt the need to offer her message in private. Tilting her head slightly, she silently requested Lara to read her thoughts and felt Lara enter her mind.

"I need you and Lord Thomas to come to the Healing Room. It is urgent!" Flora softly said.

"Please excuse me," Lara said, as she reached for Thomas' hand. "We must attend to a private matter and will be back as quickly as we can. I will leave Preston to lead the discussion regarding the surprise penetration of the Evergreen Forest and plans to prevent a future attack."

Lara led Thomas through the doorway and followed closely behind Flora. Safely away from the Council Chamber, Lara stopped and waited for Flora to face her.

"What has happened?" Lara asked, as she felt Thomas wrap his arm around her waist keeping her steady. "Has there been another attack? Has someone else been harmed?"

"No, My Lady," Flora said, as she rubbed her hand gently against Lady Lara's arm. "Do not worry. I have not received anyone else for healing." Closing her eyes for a moment to settle herself, she opened her eyes to see Lady Lara's shoulders relax. "I am sorry. I did not want to speak in front of the council."

"Do you fear a traitor amongst the council?" Thomas asked, as he felt Lara's hands begin to tremble. Feeling the need to pull his vision, he grasped her tightly and waited for her face to come into view.

"No, My Lord," Flora replied. "It is best that you see for yourself."

Thomas held Lara's hand tightly as they followed Flora through the hallway toward the Healing Room. Approaching the open doorway, they could see two shadows cast upon the stone floor out into the hallway. Stepping closer to the door, Lara could see Tate standing at the foot of Baxter's cot. Hearing the rustle of Flora's skirt, Tate turned giving a full view of Baxter sitting up on the side of the cot with his hands over his face.

"Baxter!" Lara shouted, with surprise as she moved past Tate and knelt before Baxter. "We thought we lost you. It is so nice to have you back with us."

Pulling Baxter's hands from his face, Lara watched as he opened his eyes. A deep crimson starred back at her. Softly she placed her hand on the side of his face. Baxter pulled away and hissed letting his fangs descend. Tate quickly moved to pull Lara away from the danger before her.

"He will not harm me," she said, as she stood and then sat down on the cot next to Baxter. "I can help you Baxter. I can help you control the madness."

Baxter pulled away and stood clutching his neck with both hands. Moaning from the fire in his throat, he looked about the room desperate to find a way to escape. Seeing the doorway blocked, he franticly looked about for another exit. The burning sensation worsened causing his body to shake violently. Trying to free himself from the pain in his throat, he dug his fingernails into his flesh. His screams began to fill the room, and Lady Lara started to move closer to him. Thomas grabbed her by the arms and pulled her back against his chest.

"Stay back, my love," Thomas said, as he tried to move her behind his body for protection. "He does not have control of himself."

"Thomas, I can help him as I helped you," responded Lara, as she tried to pull herself away from his hold. "He will not harm me. He needs our help."

Remembering the agony he had gone through after being turned, he let go of Lara and watched her slowly step toward Baxter. They watched Baxter back away from Lady Lara and into the corner of the room. Sliding down the wall to the stone floor, tears began to fill his eyes. Covering his face with his hands, he rested his head against his knees. Lady Lara slowly knelt down in front of Baxter and ran her hand over his soft wavy hair.

"Baxter, let me help you," Lara whispered, softly keeping her hand against the side of his face. "I can assure you that it will not be easy to let go of the madness. Once you do, the pain will be gone." She began to stroke his face trying to calm him, but he jerked from her touch. Pulling her hand back, she continued to plead with him. "You know that I have helped Thomas and Tate. You have seen that they have been able to control it. Once it is gone, it will give you great relief." Lifting his face, she could see the pain that held him. "Please trust me, Baxter. Please, we all care for you. We will not let you harm yourself or anyone else." Watching for any sign of understanding, she stood before him hoping she had gotten through to him. "If my offer pleases you, give me your name and take my hand so that you may come with me," replied Lara, as she offered her small hand to him.

Thomas and Tate stood ready to grab Lady Lara away from him if he tried to attack her. Seeing him move slightly forward, they quickly stepped closer to her. Not able to control his worry for her, Thomas placed his hands on her waist. Feeling her within his touch made him feel better, even though, the threat was still close enough to attack her.

Baxter looked up into Lady Lara's kind face, he struggled with the pain that consumed his body. He wanted to sink his fangs into her neck. He wanted to taste her blood and feel it soothe the fire in this throat. He wanted to make the fire go away. Wanting to release the pain, more than anything, and feeling helpless to do it, he slowly extended his hand as he spoke, "My name is Baxter."

Lara took hold of his pale large hand and whispered a few short words into the air. Instantly they vanished.

Knowing Lara had taken him to the Holding Room and would need Meadow, Flora quickly left the room to head toward the tower to retrieve her. Tate sat down on the cot and ran his hands through his hair. Thomas crossed the room to the cot facing Tate and sat down as he let his vision fade.

"Do you think he saw who killed him?" Thomas asked, as he looked in Tate's direction for answers.

"He was shot in the back," Tate replied. "He may not have seen anything."

"We all know it was the Black Thistle Army that did this," Thomas said, as he stood feeling frustrated over the lack of information gathered by Will and Oliver. "It had to be them. A hunter would have called for help and offered his apology."

"You are probably right," Tate responded, with a worried look upon his face. "If it was Black Thistle, they probably think he died. They know that no one was around to see it happen."

"What are you saying?" Thomas asked, as he sat back down waiting for Tate's reply.

"If Baxter is dead," Tate said, as he played the possible scenario around in his mind. "Black Thistle cannot be blamed. Baxter cannot name his killer. They do not have to prepare for retaliation. Proof would be needed to warrant an attack on Black Thistle Castle. Proof would be needed to accuse a member of their army of the attack."

"Without proof, we cannot do anything?" Thomas asked, knowing the answer he would receive from Tate, but wanting to tear Jario's head from his body.

"We cannot act without proof," replied Tate. "Cumberland Castle would come to the defense of Black Thistle Castle if we attacked. Even though we have accused Jario as a traitor and for kidnapping Lady Lara, we cannot attack the people that live at Black Thistle Castle. It would bring disgrace to Lady Lara. She would not allow it."

"Are you telling me that we standby and wait for Jario and his new army to attack us one by one?" Thomas asked, as he stood again and pulled his vision so he could look directly into Tate's face.

"I am saying we wait," replied Tate, as he stood and grasped his brother's arms. "We use Gavenia's hawk to gain more information. We patrol the forest in pairs. We look for any signs that mark a location of hiding. We make Jario think that Baxter died. The dead cannot implicate an attacker. Jario will be careless and won't be expecting us to focus on his army. Most importantly, we wait until Baxter can tell us what happened. He is our proof."

Feeling helpless but understanding Tate's point of view, Thomas wrapped his arms around his brother. He meant the world to him and appreciated his respect for Lady Lara and Evergreen. Looking at Tate's grin, Thomas said, "We need to get back to the council and let them know about Baxter. We need to prepare for the pyre that will be held in his honor."

Chapter 16

Weeks had passed since the attack on Baxter resulting in his death and eventual turning. After meeting with the council, it was decided that he would be secretly hidden away in the Holding Room during his recovery. The funeral pyre was privately attended by Lady Lara, Lord Thomas and the Evergreen Council. The council felt the appearance of Baxter's death would prevent knowledge of his turning getting back to Jario and his army. The only sign that Jario knew of Baxter's death was a note of condolence sent by messenger to Lady Lara several days after the pyre.

Taking comfort from Baxter's improvement, Tate continued to escort Gavenia to the outskirts of the Evergreen Forest. Her hawk had become a common sight around the Black Thistle Castle, and Tate did not worry as much about her safety. She frequently landed on Jario's balcony and listened to conversations he held with Buck and Gusty. Jario seemed to enjoy the presence of the white hawk and frequently left the door to the balcony open in hopes that the hawk would visit him. Since seeing it during his painful recovery from the spell offered by Gautier, he found it to be a sign of affirmation for his plans of Evergreen's destruction. He believed that the hawk had safely brought him through the pain of the spell.

On this particular outing, Gavenia had perched upon the roof of the barracks to watch the army practice and to gain a count of the growing members of the army. Her first few flights confirmed the small inexperienced army of fewer than twenty five members. Over time it had doubled in size to slightly over fifty and gained the skills needed to fight with weapons. They all appeared to be human which gave the advantage to the Evergreen Army during an evening attack, but it would make it more difficult during the bright sunlight. The count of hidden vampires would need to be gathered. She saw no way to see within the barracks and would leave this mission for another day.

Bored with the crude grunting and constant ringing of swords, Gavenia circled above the castle looking for an open window or balcony. Finding a door left open, she bravely flew through the opening to find a large room filled with banners hanging from the ceiling. Stacks of books with leather bindings lined the walls waiting to be placed upon the thick wooden shelves held by iron brackets. Perching upon an iron staff that held a brightly colored banner displaying thistles, she observed a large stone hearth that held a roaring fire. At the far end of the room, rolls of parchments were stacked upon a large wooden table. One parchment was spread open with small stones holding down each corner. Just as she was about to leave her perch for the table, Jario and Gautier entered the room followed by the white wolf.

"I tell you, the spell does not last long enough," Jario complained, as he clenched his fists. "I was visiting Magna, and my request changed before I was ready. There must be a way to make my requests last longer. I would prefer unlimited time."

Ignoring Jario's wringing hands, Gautier knelt down and stroked the thick white fur of the wolf before he spoke, "If unlimited time is what you desire, it can be done. It will have severe consequences. Understand me Jario, the consequences will be severe."

Moving toward the table and glancing at the map, he ran his finger over several markings before he turned to face Gautier. Taking a few steps toward him, he started to raise his hand to grab Gautier, but stopped as he remembered the wolf by his side.

"Yes," Jario replied, as he stepped back hearing a low growl from the wolf. "The amount of time is extremely important. I may fail without this addition to the spell. I can deal with any consequences it might inflict upon me."

Gautier was well aware of Jario's arrogance. He saw more and more of it every day. It troubled him and made him worry that his reckless actions would harm Kayleigh. This was something that he would not tolerate. He would put an end to Jario before he would allow harm to come to her.

"You realize there will be more pain involved with any physical spell," Gautier said, as he continued to stroke the wolf. "There will be more pain and more healing."

"I can deal with pain," Jario smirked, as he tried to show Gautier that he was not afraid. "I dealt with the pain the first time. I can deal with it again."

"If you are sure, go to your chamber," Gautier ordered, as he stood feeling the wolf lean against his leg. "I will meet you there at midnight. Remove your clothing and stand ready for me. I will offer you unlimited time."

Filled with excitement, Jario nodded and quickly turned toward the door leaving Gautier and the wolf standing by the warmth of the hearth. Gautier could hear him humming a tune as he walked through the hallway. Kneeling once again, he rubbed the wolf behind her ears.

"Shall we return to our chamber, my pretty little wolf," Gautier whispered, as he snuggled his face against her soft fur. "Your wolf is beautiful, but I need the feel of my beloved Kayleigh against my skin tonight."

Feeling her wet tongue lick his face, he smiled. He loved her wolf form and knew that she hid within her wolf. She feared being trapped without her wolf, again. He had to make her feel safe, and the only way to do that was to kill Velsa. He would see to Velsa's end. He would bide his time. He would surprise the old hag with her death. She would feel his revenge come to her for the binding spell that kept him away from his beloved Kayleigh. Gautier stood and left the room with the wolf following closely behind him.

Waiting for Gautier's footsteps to fade, Gavenia's hawk swooped down to view the parchment that was spread out on the table. Seeing the map and the marks drawn upon it, she knew the marks were within the Evergreen Forest. Feeling she needed to leave before someone closed the open door and trapped her inside, she flew out the door and headed back to Tate.

* * *

Tate spotted the hawk and turned Twiggs back toward Evergreen. Keeping her hawk in sight, he made his way back through the forest watching her circle and play within the wind. He knew she loved the freedom her hawk gave her, and he enjoyed listening to her descriptions of how the forest looked from the sky. Seeing her frolic above him, he sensed that she was teasing him. Trying to keep up with her, he let Twiggs weave between the trees with his arms stretched out to his sides. He laughed as he felt the air move against his body.

Is this what she feels? Why didn't I feel this sensation when I made use of my gift of great leaping? Is this feeling because I am sharing this with Gavenia?

Grabbing the reins, he gave Twiggs a nudge with his knees and felt

93

the stallion increase his speed as they raced through the forest. He wanted to be there when she stepped from the stable. He wanted to take her hand and feel the heat race through his body. He was falling in love with her and hoped she would belong to him one day.

Reaching the stable, he tethered Twiggs and waited for Gavenia. He could hear her running toward him and grabbed her by the waist twirling her into the air. Her smile was breathtaking, and his arms tingled with heat. Setting her down, she raised her face to be able to look into his eyes. Smiling, she gently leaned against his body. He wrapped his arms around her shoulders feeling her heart beat. Pulling her back, he leaned his head down watching her close her eyes and gently brushed her lips with his own. She tasted like sweet cream.

"Preston wants to see Gavenia," hollered Elda, as she began to laugh and make loud kissing noises for Tate's benefit. "Business before pleasure."

Embarrassed, Gavenia's cheeks flushed a deep rose as she looked down at her feet. Tate grabbed her hand and led her toward the castle. Elda leaned against the doorway with her arms folded. Stepping back to let them pass, she snickered as she followed closely behind them.

* * *

Gusty stood outside of Jario's door. He had orders to keep anyone but Gautier away from his chamber. Hearing heavy boots, he looked up to see the warlock approaching him. He felt the strong power radiate off of Gautier's body and could feel it increase as he came towards him. Trying not to show any fear, he nodded slightly to acknowledge his presence.

"My Lord is waiting for you," Gusty sad, as he rapped his knuckle against the door before he opened it allowing Gautier to enter Jario's chamber.

Stepping into the chamber, he looked around the room for Jario. Hearing the door close behind him, Gautier saw Jario stride naked from the bathing chamber to stand before him. He could see the scars covering Jario's body from the first spell. All spells, that changed the physical appearance of the requestor, would leave scars or deformities. He had provided power to many greedy kings and seen them turn into horrible withered creatures. Jario was power hungry and would end up like all the others.

"Are you sure you want another spell?" Gautier asked, as his eyes drifted over Jario's muscular frame. The scars did not detract from his masculine features and gave him an appearance of strength. He knew that battle scars always seemed to arouse the ladies. "It will cause additional damage to your body. Is this access to unlimited time, worth the pain and disfigurement?"

Jario paced back and forth with his eyes closed while he grabbed his chin and ran his hand slowly over his mouth. His fangs dropped, and he ran his tongue over their sharp points. He was taking a moment to weigh his options. He had failed to secure Lady Lara for his own and needed the power. Without it, he would fail again. He would endure extreme pain to have her. He would do anything to have her.

"Yes, I am sure," Jario stated, as he faced Gautier and readied himself for the spell. "The pain does not matter to me. I will suffer through it for the ability to have unlimited time."

"Prepare yourself," Gautier said, as he started to circle around Jario.

Gautier chanted in a language that Jario had never heard. Heat began to fill his body and bright lights began to flash behind his eyes. Feeling dizzy he tried to move his feet to keep from falling, but his feet would not move. Piercing pain tore through his chest and arms. He suddenly smelled smoke and feared that Magna had entered his chamber until he realized that his body was on fire. He screamed from the pain as his flesh melted. The flames licked at his face. A shriek of agony filled the chamber and then there was absolute quiet as he succumbed to the darkness.

Gautier watched as Jario's burnt body fell to the floor. Physical spells were deadly and always attacked what the person held most important. Jario's vanity had driven the spell to attack his appearance. He would be terribly scarred unless he used the power to hide it. Without the power, he would be a monster. Turning he walked toward the door to retrieve Gusty.

Opening the door he called to him, "Come take care of your master. He is badly burned and will need care. I have taken all the pain I can from him, but it still leaves him in horrific agony. Tend to his burns. He knew of the risk and wanted the power. There is nothing more I can do."

Seeing Gautier leave the chamber, Gusty stepped forward to see a charred body resting against the stone floor. Smelling the burnt flesh, he gagged as he bent down and picked up his master and laid him on the clean bed linens. Jario's eyes opened, and he grabbed Gusty's arm as he screamed, "Help me! The pain is more than I can bear!"

Chapter 17

Lara entered the Holding Room to find Baxter sitting at the table. His smile always brought her such happiness, and it was good to see him smiling again. It had been weeks since his turning, and Baxter had managed to escape the madness. His journey had not been as difficult as Thomas' or Tate's, since he had not consumed human blood, but it was still difficult. His nightmares had been filled with the pain of the arrow piercing his heart and the sense of failure. He felt shame over losing focus and letting himself be attacked.

Seeing Lady Lara, Baxter pushed from the table and stood facing her. He bowed slightly and raised his shackled hand over his heart. "My Lady, you honor me with your visit."

Taking the seat across the table from him, she nodded for him to take a seat. Seeing the brightness of his eyes, she pulled a key from her pocket and set it upon the table.

"It is time to release you from your restraints," Lara said. "Are you ready to leave this place and rejoin your friends among the army?"

"I am ready," he responded, as he lowered his head feeling shame over the attack. "I must apologize for putting Evergreen in danger. My mistake could have led to the harm of you or your people."

"Baxter, it was an attack," Lara reassured him. "The arrow could have easily found Will or Oliver. No harm came to me or my people. You have always been faithful to me and Evergreen Castle. I trust that you will always be faithful in the future."

Baxter raised his head to look into Lady Lara's eyes. He saw the sincerity he had hoped to find. Smiling he raised his hands toward her.

Lara stood and grasped Baxter's hand. Picking up the key, Baxter sighed as he heard the lock release and the cuff fall from his wrist. As he watched her take his other hand, he heard the sound of the cuff hitting the table, and it brought the same grateful sigh. Rubbing his wrists and then shaking his hands, he pushed back the chair and stood.

"Thank you is not nearly enough for what you have done for me," Baxter said, as a single tear ran down his cheek. Offering his arm to Lara, he politely said, "My Lady, may I escort you to the Command Center."

"Baxter, I would be honored," Lara replied, as she put her arm through his.

* * *

Tate led Gavenia through the door to the Command Center. Preston, Thomas and Oliver stood by a large table that was covered by several maps. Seeing her, Preston motioned for her to join them. Approaching the trio, she gave a slight curtsy to Thomas and sat down in the chair offered by Preston. Tate gave his brother a slight bow and took his place behind Gavenia's chair.

"We have been anxious to hear what you have learned about the army," Preston said, as he unrolled a map and laid stones at each corner. "Rumors have spread that Jario has been looking for volunteers to join his army, and the ships have been bringing strangers to the village."

Elda joined the men at the table. Giving Gavenia a nod of reassurance, she glanced up at Tate to see him give her a much deserved dirty look.

Feeling a little nervous, Gavenia took a deep breath before she answered Preston, "The numbers have increased to about fifty. Their skills have improved based on what I have witnessed. Several different kinds of weapons have been used during their daily training. However, I have been unable to confirm the presence of vampires since my hawk visits are during the daylight hours. It would bring suspicion if a hawk was seen during the darkness." Waiting for a comment from Preston or Thomas and hearing none she continued, "I was able to enter the castle."

Hearing her statement, Tate's back stiffened. He had warned her before her flight of the danger of entering the castle, and the chance that she could get lost or trapped.

"Can either Jario or Magna sense a shifter?" Tate directed his question to Elda. "We know nothing of the warlock or the wolf and their powers. If they sense her, they would try to capture her."

She would never survive the torture that Magna would inflict upon her for her escape, he thought.

97

"They did not sense me. Jario, the warlock, and the wolf were all in the chamber, and they did not sense my presence," she responded, with a smile. Turning her head to look up at Tate, she saw the worried look upon his face. "I heard Jario complaining about the spell that Gautier granted him. He complained that it did not last long enough. He wanted unlimited time."

"Unlimited time for what?" Thomas asked, as he looked at the others hoping they knew what she was talking about.

"I am not sure, My Lord," Gavenia said, as she rubbed her damp palms against each other and then along the sides of her breeches. "Jario speaks in riddles. He said that he was visiting Magna, and his request changed before he was ready. He wanted it to last longer. He wanted unlimited time."

Everyone started to laugh and snicker. Suddenly understanding why everyone was laughing, Gavenia's face flushed, and she covered her face with her hands.

"He needs help to bed Magna," Elda said, as she shook her head and rolled her eyes. "I constantly heard tales of how he pleasured women to the brink of their undoing. I heard more tales than I care to count. He bragged about every single encounter. Either he lied, or Magna is too much for him to handle."

"It has to be something else, but what?" Thomas asked. "Lady Lara spoke of him trying to control his arousal when he held her captive. He held back. This just doesn't make sense."

"What else did you hear?" Preston asked, as he knelt down before her. Taking her small hands in his, he rubbed his thumb back and forth to calm her nerves.

Unprepared for the feelings of jealousy, Tate placed his hand upon Gavenia's shoulder and gave Preston a look of warning. Preston stood and stepped back away from Gavenia. Tate was uncomfortable about his closeness to her, and Preston could see it in Tate's eyes. Raising his hands slightly to offer a silent apology, he saw Tate nod in acceptance.

Uncomfortable with the sudden silence, Gavenia brought her hand to her mouth and coughed to gain their attention. "The warlock sent Jario to his chamber," she said, as she looked directly at Preston trying to control her nerves. "He told him he would perform the spell at midnight, to give him unlimited time. He also told him, there would be pain and damage to his body."

"We need you to go back to Black Thistle Castle tomorrow and find out what happened to Jario," Preston said, as he carefully watched Tate for a reaction. "We need to know what the spell allows him to do."

"Jario leaves the door to his chamber open for me," she said, as she stood from her chair glancing at Tate fearing his reaction. "When he sees me on the balcony, he speaks of how I saved him from the pain. I will go to his chamber tomorrow, but I must rest tonight. My mind is weary, and I need my strength to transition into my hawk."

"Of course," Preston said. "Before you go, was there anything else that you noticed that might help us plan for an attack?"

"I almost forgot," she gasped and hurried toward the maps on the table. "There was a map spread out on the table similar to this one. It had places marked in the Evergreen Forest, as well as, places marked in the Black Thistle courtyard. Lines were drawn between some of the marks. What do you think they were?"

Oliver had been quiet up until hearing about the marks in the forest.

"Damn! We saw rocks stacked upon each other and assumed that hunters had marked good hunting areas" he said. "I made no connection between the markers and Baxter's death until now. These markers must be related to the marks on their maps. The lines between the marks must be marking tunnels. What else could they be? That is how Baxter's attacker got away from us without us seeing him."

"Oliver, take some men and survey the area where Baxter was attacked," Preston ordered. "If there are tunnels, we need to find them. Do not enter them. Your scent would be noticed by their vampires. They would know that their plot had been discovered. Post guards at the tunnels. There might be a chance that we can capture their spies."

Turning to look at Gavenia, he kept Tate in view out of the corner of his eye. "Gavenia, you have served us well. Get some rest and prepare your hawk for tomorrow."

Nodding she turned to Thomas and curtsied. Gavenia looked up at Thomas and smiled as she bid him a good evening, "My Lord."

Tate gave his brother a quick bow and took Gavenia's arm to lead her from the Command Center and back to her chamber. Feeling the heat race up his arm, he let the tension leave his body and the calm take over. Halfway to her chamber, he heard her sigh as she began to sway. Bending down and lifting her into his arms, he carried her the rest of the way to her chamber. He felt her head rest against his chest and delighted in the warmth of their closeness. Arriving at her chamber door, he sat her feet upon the floor and helped her stand.

"Rest peacefully this evening," Tate whispered, as he brushed a lock of hair from her face and gazed into the brilliant green of her eyes. "We will have a long day tomorrow."

Standing on her tiptoes, she kissed his lips and felt him wrap his arms around her waist pulling her closer. Her body warmed as he returned the kiss. Feeling him take her shoulders and break their warm embrace, he turned her toward the door. Not wanting the evening to end, she leaned her head back against his chest.

"My little hawk, you need your rest," Tate whispered, softly as he nuzzled her neck. "I don't want to leave you, but I will not be able to control myself if I stay any longer. I will have sweet dreams of you and return for you in the morning."

As she reached for the door, she turned to look at him one last time, "Tate, I will dream of you too."

Watching her enter her chamber and slowly close the door, his body wanted to explode with the love he felt for her. Bending over and grabbing his knees, he tried to calm himself. The rush of heat he felt when they touched lingered on his skin. It use to leave his body when they separated, but he noticed that it remained with him, long after she would leave him.

If this was not meant to be, I would not have been able to bring her back to Evergreen, he thought. I would not feel happiness when I look upon her face. I would not love her. I do love her.

Reassured that fate must have brought them together, he felt heat surge in his chest as he straightened his back. Energized by the feeling, he sped through the hallways as he made his way back to the Command Center.

* * *

Oliver was the first to see Baxter and Lady Lara enter the Command Center. He sheathed his sword and ran toward them as he shouted Baxter's name. Stopping, briefly, to bow and place his hand over his chest before Lady Lara, he grabbed Baxter by the shoulders and pulled him into a bear hug. Hearing Oliver's shouts, Thomas pulled his vision to see the new vampire standing among his army and friends.

"It is good to have you back, my friend," Oliver said, as he hugged him for second time, while slapping his back a little too eagerly. "We have missed you. I'm afraid that several members of the army have been slacking while you were recovering."

"I will make sure things are back to normal," Baxter said, as he grinned and looked around to acknowledge everyone. "You all know that I could best most of you before I turned. I would imagine that I am a force to be feared now that I am a vampire."

Hearing everyone laugh was music to his ears. Once he had been able to calm most of the madness, he began to miss his friends. He was grateful to have them all back, again.

"Enough of this joviality, I want to hear about your plans to capture the bastard that shot me when my back was turned," Baxter snarled.

Waiting patiently for the crowd around Baxter to resume their training, Preston beckoned Baxter over to the wall displaying several maps. Lady Lara followed closely behind Baxter and stepped next to Thomas placing her hand within his.

"You were missed my friend," Preston said, as he put a hand upon Baxter's shoulder. "When you are ready, Elda will take you to the Room of Powers. We need to know what gifts you have been given."

"I hear we have a new vampire among us," shouted Tate, as he ran to Baxter's side. "You certainly went out of your way to join us."

Elbowing Baxter in the stomach, the two vampires began to wrestle with one another until Thomas took hold of Tate's arm.

"We have work to do," Thomas sternly said. "Baxter needs to be informed of what has transpired since his absence."

Feeling the seriousness of Thomas' voice, Tate and Baxter returned their focus back to Preston. Baxter watched as Preston circled the area where he had been attacked. Hearing the discussions about markers and tunnels, Baxter's mind flew back to the man that stood before him with the brand upon his chest.

Baxter held up his hand to interrupt Preston, "I surprised a man with the mark of Black Thistle Castle upon his chest. He said that he was hunting for food and appeared to be alone, but I doubted he was telling the truth. Before I could subdue him, I took an arrow through the back. I never saw who attacked me."

"We have our confirmation," Preston said, as he looked at Lord Thomas. "It was an attack by the Black Thistle Army. If we need additional men to defend Evergreen, Cumberland Castle will support us, without question."

"If you don't mind, I am a little anxious to find out if I have powers?" Baxter said, as he looked at Preston and Thomas. "I see Elda standing by the door. I am ready."

"Elda," shouted Preston giving her a flick of his head to join them.

"Commander," stated Elda. "You have need of me?"

"Take Baxter to the Room of Powers," he ordered. "He is anxious, and we are curious about his powers."

"If he has any?" Elda snickered, as she jabbed Baxter in the ribs. "Follow me. If nothing happens, do not blame me."

Baxter rolled his eyes at Elda and gave her a push in the back, "Hurry up, the Commander gave you an order."

Elda sped from the room with Baxter right on her heels. He was enjoying his new speed and was anxious to find out what other enhancements were afforded to him.

* * *

Standing before the door, Elda explained, "This is the Room of Powers. It contains all the powers that could be gifted to a vampire. We are here to find out what has been gifted to you; however, know that not all vampires are gifted powers. Do not be disappointed if you receive none, because sometimes they come later." She smiled at Baxter, but she was trying to keep a serious look upon her face. "The sound you hear are from the Wispets that protect the Room of Powers. They are guardians of the gifts. They take care of the powers and make certain they stay strong. Wispets are not prisoners here in this room and can leave through a portal inside the chamber at any time they choose. They come and go, but are always present when the Wispet Queen performs the Gifting Ceremony." Elda took hold of the large elaborate handle and looked at Baxter, "Are you ready to see what gifts you might receive?"

Baxter nodded and stepped into the small chamber. Elda followed right behind him and closed the door. The light in the room was dim, but Baxter was surprised how well he could see. There were only a few small candles burning about the stone walls, and it looked like daylight. Before him was a smooth stone pillar. He had heard of the pillar and the strange words chiseled into the top of the stone. Looking about the room, he could see small clear globes lining the wooden shelves and flickering lights darting among them. A few vampires had tried to explain the room to him, but none of them could describe the magical feeling it possessed.

A warm light glowed above the pillar, and an image of a woman began to appear. She was tiny and dressed in a flowing gown of white embroidered with threads of green and lavender, just like Thomas had described. Her eyes were the brightest emerald green and filled with flecks of gold. Her lavender hair hung in ringlets about her shoulders. He noticed the beautiful crown of bright gems that sat against her forehead, just above her eyes.

"Step forward Baxter," she spoke softly and motioned him forward with her hand. "Step forward and place your hands upon the pillar."

Baxter stepped forward and placed his hands upon the flat surface of the pillar. As he did, the pillar began to warm beneath his hands. The globes about the room began to glow, as well. One at a time, six globes moved to the surface of the pillar and huddled next to each other. The sound of laughter and singing could be heard about the room. Smiling, the Wispet Queen brought her finger to her mouth to hush the noise.

As the room became quiet, he watched as she touched the first globe lightly, and it began to brighten to the color of the evergreens about the castle. A word floated above the pillar. "Compulsion," she announced, as he watched the word disappear into the globe causing the globe to shake upon the pillar until she gently stroked the top of its smooth surface.

She touched the next globe lightly, and it began to spin. The Queen's hair began to move about from a slight breeze. Watching the blurry white globe, a word floated above the pillar. "Wind," she announced, as the spinning globe slowly came to a stop.

She stroked the next globe, and it began to blink. One moment it was aqua, and the next it was gone. Continuing to blink, a word floated above the pillar. "Flash," she announced, as he watched the word disappear into the globe, and the blinking stopped.

Touching the next globe, it appeared to be black with gold starbursts inside. The globe jumped slightly with each burst of light. "Read Thoughts," she said, as she waved her hand over the globe and it hummed softly before it faded.

Touching the next globe, it changed quickly into a bright orange. Baxter could feel heat. "Hands of Fire," she said, as she waved her hand over the globe, and it instantly cooled and faded.

As she touched the last globe, it began to brighten. The brightness made him close his eyes, and he wanted to use his hand to help shield them. "Walk in Daylight," she said, as he heard a slight sizzle before the light dimmed, and he could finally open his eyes.

"These six gifts have been given," declared the Wispet Queen, as she looked directly into Baxter's eyes. "Use them well."

The Wispet Queen faded from view as the chatter and laughter increased for a moment and then diminished, returning the room in dim candlelight. The globes floated into the air and swirled about Baxter's head. One by one, they returned to their place upon the shelves.

Turning around, Baxter looked at Elda. She gave him a wink and opened the door.

"We need to report back to Preston," she said, as she waited for Baxter to exit the room. "You have some strong gifts. Training will be required for the gift of wind. We don't want a storm to rage inside the castle."

Overwhelmed, Baxter followed Elda through the hallway. He had new talents that could be valuable to Evergreen, and he needed to master them quickly. He hoped he had enough time to learn how to use them before Black Thistle attacked.

Chapter 18

Hours had passed since Gautier offered the spell that set Jario's body on fire. The severe pain had caused him to slip in and out of consciousness. Even though vampires had the ability to heal themselves, the trauma to his body was well beyond anything he had ever suffered. He had given up opening and closing his eyes due to the extreme pain of moving his eyelids over the blisters on his eyes.

Gusty had spent hours trying to relieve his pain with cool damp cloths and an organic salve given to him by an old woman that was new to the castle. The salve smelled like rat droppings, and it did nothing more than add to the pain by stinging where Gusty smeared it on his body. Jario was helpless, and Gusty feared that he would succumb to the extreme nature of the spell.

As the sun began to rise, Jario's body seemed to calm. The moans were replaced with a gurgling within his throat that sounded similar to snoring. The blistered and blackened flesh that covered his body showed signs of beginning to heal. Crackling sounds of his charred skin breaking open as his body twitched was unnerving. Pieces of charred flesh began to fall from his body, filling the chamber with the scent of death and decay. Finally, Jario seemed to be resting quietly.

Pulling the heavy drapes back from the balcony doors, Gusty opened a narrow stained glass door to let in the cool morning breeze. He was careful to only open the door that would not allow sunlight to spill upon Jario's bed. Gusty stood for a moment and let the fresh air cool his body. Needing a break from the moaning and the stench, he quietly made his way to the door and left the chamber.

* * *

Gavenia's hawk circled the castle waiting for Jario's balcony door to be opened. Seeing the glint of sunlight against the glass door as it moved, she slowly descended to the balcony wall. She could hear what sounded like brittle parchment being crushed, as well as, Jario's snoring. Cautiously, she moved to allow herself to peer through the open door. Not hearing any voices, she flew into the chamber. Perching on the back of a tall wooden chair close to Jario's bed, she could see something dark within the bed linens. At first, she was confused.

Why would he put a smoldering log within the bed linens of this grand bed?

Suddenly, the realization of what was before her made her hawk ruffle her feathers and squawk in fear. The warlock's spell had burned Jario beyond recognition. The foul stench of burning flesh still lingered in the air. Feeling the need to leave the horrible sight, she lifted her wings to take flight.

"My lovely hawk has returned," Jario uttered, with a raspy voice. More blackened skin fell from his face as he spoke. "You have come to heal me. I fear I am close to my final death. I need you to stay with me. Your beauty will be the last thing I see before I leave this world."

Tilting her head, she listened carefully to Jario's words. With each movement, the charred flesh fell from Jario's body revealing the red raw skin beneath. Seeing him close his eyes, she flew to the post at the foot of his bed to draw his attention. She needed to keep him talking.

"You are concerned for me," he coughed uncontrollably and raised his hand to his mouth. Watching large chunks of blackened flesh fall from his arm, tears began to fall from his eyes as he mumbled. "Once I am stronger, I can fix this. Do not be afraid of me. I can fix this. You will see, I will be able to make myself appear strong and handsome again. You will be amazed at the power I have been given from Gautier. I can show you, but I need to rest and heal. I have had enough torture and need to sleep." Closing his eyes, he drifted off and began to snore.

Seeing enough, she flew from the chamber and away from Black Thistle Castle.

He spoke of torture. Torture? I have heard him speak of torture before this day, she thought, *as she flew toward Evergreen.*

Not waiting for Tate to acknowledge her return, she sped as fast as she could through the air back to Evergreen. Gliding through the open stable doors and into the stall, she transitioned back to her human form and knelt in the soft straw as she gasped for air. Feeling the comfort of air filling her lungs, she reached for the linen tunic and pulled it over her head. Tears welled in her eyes and caused her to stumble as she tried to step into her breeches. Tying the leather laces, she saw the ground spin about her feet causing her to sway. Grabbing the stall gate to keep herself from falling, she replayed everything she had seen, over in her mind.

Why didn't I wait for Tate? I should have gone to him. I need him to hold me and take away the horrible visions I see in my mind. Visions of blood and darkness. Visions of chains, dungeons and torture.

As she stepped from the stable, the sound of Twiggs' hoofs racing across the pasture, filled her ears. Seeing Gavenia, Tate jumped from Twiggs' back and ran toward her.

"Are you hurt?" he asked, as he ran his eyes over her body looking for a wound. Seeing none, he noticed the tears upon her cheeks and wrapped his arms around her, pulling her against his body. "It will be alright. I will make it alright." He kissed the top of her head and held her while she sobbed.

"I remember being in the dungeon, Tate" she whispered, as she felt her body begin to shake. "I remember all the pain, blood and torture. I remember Magna and Jario."

Tate's body began to stiffen. He held on to Gavenia with all his might and feared what she would say next.

"Oh my God, I remember you. Tate, I remember you." Gavenia cried, as she looked up at Tate and tried to push away from him, but Tate held her tight against his body.

"I will tell you all I remember," Tate whispered, as he closed his eyes praying she would forgive him. "If you remember everything, you know that I was a prisoner too. Please give me a chance to explain. Do not condemn me without letting me explain."

The look of hatred filled her eyes as she continued to push against his chest. Finally, he released her from his grasp. She stepped back and ran toward the castle. He dropped to his knees, as he watched her run away from him.

* * *

It had taken weeks for Jario to fully recover from the spell. His body was permanently scarred, and he had lost an ear, all of his fingers, and all of his hair. Thankfully, his manhood was still intact and in working order. He made a habit of frequently reaching between his legs to confirm it.

The ability to use the spell with unlimited time hid his monstrous appearance from everyone. He could hide it all, except the headaches that plagued him. His first headache had occurred when the torches were set ablaze in the courtyard, and he had panicked in front of his army. Seeing the hearth in his room come to life with red and orange flames sent him running to the bathing chamber holding his head until Gusty could smother the flames. This caused Jario to ban all flames from his presence. Since most rooms within the castle required torches for light, Jario ordered that all meetings be held during the daylight hours. Care was taken to avoid direct sunlight and all hearths were to be left empty.

Anxious to hear from Buck about the army's numbers and strength, he sent word to have Buck and Gusty meet him in his chamber. Even with all the pain and suffering, he had not forgotten about his desire for Lady Lara and the destruction of Evergreen. It was time to make good on his desires. Hearing heavy boots outside his door, he shouted for them to enter as soon as he heard them rap upon the door.

"Come in, come in," Jario shouted, as he moved to his chair at the head of the table. He had recently moved the large table into his chamber for private meetings. Sitting down, he motioned for the men to sit. "Tell me about my army."

Gripping the back of the chair and pulling it from the table, Gusty seated himself and watched Buck do the same. They both knew of his power to request change, first hand, and they were glad he was not sitting before them in his true appearance.

Buck shifted in his chair before he spoke, "We have enlisted ninety men into your army. Sixty are skilled with multiple weapons. Five men have gone to Magna requesting to be turned. She has turned them and will turn all that ask it of her. Two rogue vampires have recently joined your army, and they have been put in charge of the new vampires."

"You have increased the numbers. This is good," Jario responded, with a smirk. Running his fingers over the top of the table, he paused and then looked at Gusty. "When will they be ready to attack Evergreen?"

"The tunnels are in good order, and the men are preparing to scout the forest. Since the killing of a member of the Evergreen Army, we want to be cautious. We don't want to walk into a trap," replied Gusty.

"You did not answer my question," Jario shouted, as he pounded his fist upon the table. "When will they be ready to attack Evergreen?"

"In four days, My Lord," Gusty quickly answered and pushed back from the table. "They will be ready in four days."

There is no way that this army is ready to attack Evergreen, he thought. If he hears anything less than four days from me, my final death will be handed to me.

"Good," Jario replied, as he stood from the table knocking over his chair. "Do you have plans to bring Lady Lara to me? She must be unharmed. Also, I want her new mate. I promised Thomas to Magna."

"A small army will use the tunnels to gain access to the Evergreen Forest. From there they will storm the castle and draw the Evergreen Army out into the open. Another group of men will attack from the cliffs. Two vampires are tasked to find Lady Lara. Lord Thomas should be close to her, and this will allow them to take both of them prisoner, barring any protection spells."

"This is excellent," Jario exclaimed, as he paced back and forth before setting his chair upright and seating himself. "Let me know when you are ready to make your way to Evergreen. I will make preparations for our visitors."

Feeling the need to rid themselves of him, Gusty and Buck hurried toward the door. Looking over their shoulder for any last minute comments, they were relieved to see Jario walking toward the balcony. They quickly left the chamber and ran toward the barracks.

Seeing a small shadow on the stone floor, Jario slowly pulled the door to the balcony back to reveal the shadow of his precious hawk perched on the balcony wall. He had hoped he would receive a visit, now that he was well.

"You have come to see me. My beautiful hawk, I am happy to see you," Jario cooed, softly from behind cover of the door. "You watched over me during my recovery, and I have escaped my final death because of your visits. Would you join me?"

Gavenia's hawk was cautious. She had heard the men talking and already had the information she needed for the Evergreen Army, but she needed to see him. The last time she had seen Jario he was nothing more than a mass of blisters and charred flesh. Evergreen still needed to know the power of the spell.

Lifting her wings, she flew into the chamber and perched upon the tall post of the bed. Shock made her ruffle her feathers. He held no scars from his ordeal. He was completely well. She carefully watched him as he moved away from the door and toward the bed.

Thank goodness, he left the door open, she thought.

"You honor me with your visit," Jario said, as he bowed deeply with his arms out wide.

Playing along, she dipped her head in response. She watched him smile and clap his hands with glee.

"Because of you, I am whole again. You will always be welcome at Black Thistle Castle," he said, as he clasped his hands together under his chin. "I think I will add the hawk to my banners as a way to honor you."

She watched him pace back and forth across the chamber. He appeared to be struggling with a thought.

"I would like to keep you with me, but I will not," he whispered. "I will allow you to leave and hope for another visit."

Her hawk dipped her head again and spread her wings. She wanted to show him that she was strong and not the weak woman that he and Magna had tortured in the dungeon. She wanted to scratch his eyes out before she left, but she lifted from the post and flew out the door.

Hopefully, I will never have to return to this dreadful place, she thought. If I do, I hope it is to watch his final death.

As he watched the hawk leave his chamber and dance upon the wind, he felt a short moment of sadness. It was quickly overshadowed by the anticipation of Lady Lara's arrival and the attack on Evergreen.

"Waiting four days for her arrival is too long a wait. I do not think I can wait that long to have Lady Lara in my presence," he whispered.

Leaving his chamber, he stepped through the dark hallways. Careful to stay within their shadows, Jario made his way to the training area door. Sheltered from the sun, he stood under the broad arch of the doorway. Jario took in the number of men that had enlisted in his army. Their abilities had greatly improved since his last visit. Hearing the clashing of swords, he searched for Buck. Noticing him on the other side of the field between two of the barracks, he shouted to draw his attention. Seeing Buck's acknowledgement, he waited for Buck to approach him.

"Yes, My Lord," Buck said, as he bowed, fearing his unexpected visit.

"I have decided to move the attack up," Jario replied, as he clasped his hands behind his back. "I have changed my mind. I would like you to attack Evergreen in three days. Adjust your plans accordingly. Four days it too long. I want you to attack in three days."

Chapter 19

Hearing the news of the coming attack, the Evergreen Army was busy preparing their defensive plan. The warning towers were manned and filled with arrows, dried food, and water. Additional roosts were built in the treetops to provide advance warning of the attack. The pits that held stakes were cleaned of debris and concealed. The Command Center was busy readying the weapons and listening to Preston discuss strategy. Gavenia's hawk had been circling the castle and the surrounding area to warn of any intruders.

Lady Lara made sure the few children that lived at the castle were moved to families within the village for their protection. Flora and Niobe prepared the Healing Room with extra linens, bandages and healing ointments. A small chamber had been converted from a meeting area to provide room for more cots for the wounded. Tate helped Woodward fill the food stores with meat and blood. The garden had been cleared of all that could be harvested, and Charlotte was busy storing it all in the cold cellar. Wooden shutters had been removed and replaced with metal shields and heavy drapes had been removed to guard against flaming arrows. Fearing another attempt against Lady Lara, Thomas insisted Meadow create a new protection spell to keep anyone from taking Lady Lara from the grounds.

At the end of day two, the castle was ready and waiting for the attack. Gavenia's hawk had done a great service to Evergreen. Even though she was against returning to Black Thistle Castle after remembering her ordeal, she had agreed to make one more attempt at retrieving information before she locked herself away in her chamber. It had proved to be worthwhile, and it provided the necessary warning to prevent the fall of Evergreen.

Tate sat on the stone floor outside Gavenia's door. She had run from him after remembering the torture. The torture he had helped Magna and Jario inflict upon her body. He had tried knocking upon her door, but she would not open the door after hearing his voice. With his eyes closed and his head against the stone wall, he felt lost. The warmth he had felt was slowly fading from his body.

Determined to have her hear his side of the story, he moved his body in front of the door. Speaking loud enough for her to hear him, he told her the story of his arrival back to Echo Bluff. He explained how Magna had gotten him drunk and flashed him back to the Black Thistle dungeon to torture him for his blood. He described the pain he felt when he saw her body tortured. His eyes filled with tears as he explained how hard he fought Magna's compulsion, and how the compulsion led to his assistance in her torture. Wiping the tears from his face, he thought of Gavenia's kiss and how it tasted of sweet cream.

Gavenia, please listen to my words, he thought. They are the truth.

He paused for a moment to collect his thoughts. He carefully described the night that Magna turned him into a vampire, which led to his escape and him killing innocent people. Covering his face with his hands, he leaned down between his knees. His shoulders shuddered with his sobs for the innocents. It was then that he heard her step toward the door and sit upon the floor.

Thank goodness, she is listening to me. Please keep listening to me.

Tate leaned his head back against the door as he continued. He told her how his brother had found him and how Lady Lara had saved him. He described the journey to Black Thistle Castle with Oliver and Will to save her from the dungeon and of seeing Magna. He looked at his hands, as he described burning Magna's arm off. Pausing to wipe the tears from his face, Tate watched his hands begin to shake. Remembering how Gavenia looked when he found her in the dungeon caused him to sob and his chest to ache.

Regaining his resolve, he told her of sitting by her side in the Healing Room waiting for her to wake from her long sleep, and the joy he felt when she opened her eyes. He told her about the pleasure he felt when he saw her hawk for the first time, and the happiness it brought her. He smiled, as he tried to explain how he felt after their first kiss and his need to protect her from harm. Finally, he spoke of his love for her.

Tate stood and leaned the side of his face against her door hoping she understood everything he had told her. Hearing nothing but her breathing, he slowly backed away from the door prepared to leave.

"Gavenia, I am sorry that I hurt you," Tate said, as he placed his palms against her door. "I have said all that I can say to make you understand. If this is to be the end of us, tell me to my face. I will honor your wishes."

Silence was her only response. Standing perfectly still, Tate listened for the unlatching of the door. He could hear her stand and place her hand upon the handle. It seemed like forever before she finally opened the door and stood before him. He could see the tears upon her flushed cheeks and the redness of her eyes.

"Is this the end?" Tate asked, as he studied her face. "Is it all over for us?"

She stepped forward and lifted her face to his. Wiping a tear from her cheek, she looked into his eyes, as she spoke, "I forgive you."

Not knowing what her response really meant, Tate stood frozen in place. He forced his arms to stay at his side, for fear he would upset her.

"Your torture was as awful as mine," she spoke, through her sniffles. "I remembered everything that happened, but I did not understand everything. I am grateful that you saved me from the dungeon. I would have surely died there among the rats." A little smile crossed her face and it made him hope. "If you will forgive me for doubting you, it would make me very happy."

"Forgive you?" he choked, as he placed his fingers under her chin. "You have done nothing wrong. It is me that needs forgiveness. I kept it all from you. I should have told you everything long ago."

"Can we start over?" she asked, as she tilted her head. "I would like to forget all the sadness. I just want your love, Tate. I just want you."

Smiling broadly, Tate picked her up in his arms and nuzzled her ear as he whispered, "You may have all of me and all my love forever."

Placing her back upon her feet, Tate knelt down on one knee. "My sweet Gavenia, I love you above all others. Will you do me the honor of becoming my mate for all eternity?"

Kneeling down to place a kiss upon his cheek, Gavenia smiled as she answered his question. "I love you above all others. Yes, I will be honored to become your mate for all eternity."

Tate pulled a gold bracelet from his pouch. It was engraved with feathers and sprinkled with emeralds to match the color of her eyes. She watched as he placed it upon her wrist. Rubbing her fingers over the feathers, she could feel her hawk's loving approval.

"It is beautiful, Tate," she said, as she threw her arms around his neck. "I will cherish it always."

* * *

That evening, Tate informed Lady Lara and his brother of his proposal and Gavenia's acceptance. Thomas hugged his brother and offered his best wishes for their future together. Taking Gavenia's hand within his own, Thomas kissed the back of her hand and welcomed her to the family. Lady Lara held Gavenia's wrist as she admired the beautiful bracelet.

"I am so happy for you," Lara said, as she hugged her tightly. "I am honored to have you as my sister."

Blushing, Gavenia responded, "It is my honor, My Lady."

"Let's tell the others. They need something to lighten the mood," Thomas said, as he led them to the Command Center.

Seeing everyone huddled in groups, Thomas and Lara walked to the center of the room followed by Tate and Gavenia. Standing, everyone gathered around them waiting for a serious announcement.

"Since we are all thinking about the coming attack upon Evergreen, I wanted you to pause for a moment and think about those you care about. We all fight to protect our loved ones. I know I would do anything to protect the ones I love, and I know you would as well. It has come to my attention that we have a couple that has discovered this same love. My brother, Tate, has asked Gavenia to become his mate," Thomas announced, as he was interrupted before he could finish.

"And, she said yes," Tate shouted. "She actually said yes!"

Gavenia blushed, as everyone in the room cheered. Stepping back from the couple, Thomas wrapped his arms around Lara and kissed her softly upon her lips.

"I love you, my sweet," Thomas whispered. "I am glad that you will be mine, forever. I would do anything to protect you from harm."

"I love you too," Lara responded, as she stepped up on her tiptoes to place a kiss upon his nose. "You are everything to me."

They stood and watched as one after another offered their congratulations to Tate and Gavenia. Enjoying the smiles, laughter and love, Thomas and Lara walked around the room looking at all of their faithful friends.

"Thomas, I need to go check on Mona and Arrow," Lara said, as she pulled from Thomas' embrace. "I want to make sure they are secure."

"I will go. You stay here and enjoy the fun," Thomas said, as he kissed her lips. "I will be right back, and then, I plan to show you how much I love you."

Lara watched him leave the Command Center for the stables. Thinking of his return, she felt a tingling in her stomach. Smiling to herself, she rejoined the happy couple.

* * *

Thomas opened the stable door and headed toward the stall at the far end of the stable. He could hear the colt kicking his hoofs against the stall gate. Peering over the gate, Mona nuzzled his face with her nose. She had become sweet on him since the birth of Arrow. Seeing that all was in order with Mona and the colt, he secured the latch on the gate. Stepping from the stall, he turned to head back to the Command Center.

"Lara, you didn't have to come after me," he said, as he walked toward her.

"I missed you," she said, as she held out her hands to him.

Thomas took her hands and kissed her lips. Hearing footsteps behind him, Thomas turned to see Tolin stepping from his small quarters.

"Do you have need of me, sir?" Tolin asked, as he hung a rope upon an iron hook next to Mona's stall.

"No, I was checking on Mona and Arrow," Thomas replied, still holding her hands. "They are secure. You may retire for the evening."

"Good evening, sir," Tolin said, as he turned to go back to his room.

"Let's go back inside," Thomas said, as he turned to lead Lara back to the castle.

"Yes, let's go," she said, as they vanished into a wisp of red smoke.

* * *

The Command Center hummed with the sounds of laughter. Tate felt his cheeks beginning to ache from the constant smile upon his face. Looking down at Gavenia, he saw the soft blush on her face and happiness in her eyes. She had been able to leave the pain and suffering behind and willingly grasp hold of a future with him. He knew he could make her happy and would spend eternity showing her how much he loved her.

Seeing Lady Lara standing alone, Tate caught Baxter's eye and tilted his head in her direction. Making his way through the crowd, Baxter greeted Lady Lara with a smile.

"My Lady, where is Lord Thomas?" Baxter asked, as he looked among the faces gathered around the room.

"He has gone to the stable to make sure Mona and Arrow are secure," Lara replied, as she looked toward the doorway. "I should have moved them to a farmer's barn to keep them safe."

Placing her hands upon her stomach, the tingle she felt earlier returned. Noticing the worried expression upon Lady Lara's face, Baxter asked, "Are you ill? Do you need assistance?" Seeing her sway, he lightly grasped her arm to steady her. "Let's find a chair."

Suddenly, Baxter felt Lady Lara's body begin to tremble. Bending over to wrap his other arm around her body to keep her from falling, he looked among the crowd for help. Seeing Lady Lara stumble, Elda ran to her aide. Taking her other arm, Elda helped Baxter maneuver Lady Lara to a nearby bench.

Embarrassed, Lara lifted her hand to her forehead, "I have the strangest feeling. I haven't felt this way since . . . my sister . . . Oh no, I feel Magna's presence. Magna is here at Evergreen. Is Thomas back from the stable? Find Thomas, he could be in danger."

Elda and Baxter ran for the stable. Oliver saw them flee through the door and ran after them. Throwing the stable door open, they could see the aisle between the stalls was empty.

"Lord Thomas," Baxter shouted, looking for any sign of him. "Are you here?"

Hearing no response, Elda began to help Baxter search the stalls. As Oliver entered the stable, he stood paralyzed in place. Dread filled his mind as his eyes focused on a dwindling wisp of red smoke.

"Magna has taken Lord Thomas," he uttered, as he made a fist and smashed it through the planks of the nearest stall gate. "I have seen this red smoke before, and it belongs to the evil bitch."

Chapter 20

Thomas was sprawled face down on the cold stone floor of the Black Thistle's dungeon. Lifting his head, he felt the room spin. Resting his head back upon the floor, he waited for the room to come to a stop. He had never been able to deal with flashing. It knocked him unconscious every time Lara took him with her.

"You are awake," a deep voice mingled with the motion of the room. "I am happy that you could join me."

Pushing his body up from the floor to see the face that spoke to him, he felt the weight of heavy chains upon his arms. He attempted to pull his vision, but it blurred the features of the face before him.

"Where am I," Thomas asked, as he staggered toward the voice.

"You are a visitor of the Black Thistle Castle," the deep voice responded. "These are your new accommodations. I suggest you rest. I hear that Magna has some interesting things planned for you."

Not recognizing the voice, Thomas listened for any sound that would reveal his captor. He heard nothing but the sound of water dripping from above his head and someone breathing. Turning his body toward the breathing, he heard a deep sigh and then heavy boots upon the stone floor as they strode away from him.

Stretching his arms out, Thomas felt the bars of his cell. Grasping his hands around the metal bars, he pulled with all his might. They stood firm. Realizing they had probably been spelled, like those in Evergreen, he leaned his head against the cold metal.

Closing his eyes, he let his mind drift to Lara. He had seen her in the stable and feared she was held somewhere within the castle. Trying again

116

to pull his vision, his eyes were met with a gray cloudy fog. Either he still had not recovered from the flash, or he had been spelled to prevent him using his gifts. Frustrated and worried, he stepped back toward the rough stone wall and sat down to think of a way out.

* * *

Jario sat in the moonlight of his private balcony thinking about what tomorrow would bring. He felt sure of his plan to destroy Evergreen. It had been all he had thought about since deciding to kidnap Lady Lara for his own. Even though his first attempt had failed, he was sure his new plan would work. He had gathered men for his army and made sure they were trained. Vampires had joined the ranks and took responsibility in training those men that wanted to be turned. The tunnels to Evergreen Forest had been found passable. Lady Lara's quarters had been prepared and waited for her arrival. There was nothing left to do but wait.

The sound of boots rang through the hallway toward Jario's door. Hearing the relentless pounding upon the door, Jario yanked the door open wide.

"My Lord, something has happened," Buck said, as he squirmed at the doorway facing Jario. "Magna has brought Lord Thomas to the dungeon."

"She what!" shouted Jario, as he exited his chamber and stormed through the dark hallway. "Where is she? I will take her head for this."

"She is in the Grand Hall with a new dressmaker," Buck responded.

"Magna won't be in need of a dressmaker when I am finished with her," he growled. "I fear she has ruined our plans for an attack tomorrow. Ready the army, we will attack on my order."

"Yes My Lord," Buck replied, as he turned and ran for the barracks.

* * *

Smashing through the doors of the Grand Hall, Jario felt his fangs descend and the need to rip her limb from limb. Glaring at Magna, he motioned for the dressmaker to leave the chamber. While waiting for the door to close behind her, he watched as Magna stepped from a stool and faced him. She smoothed the folds of her dress and straightened the fine lace that gathered at her pale shoulders.

"My Lord, you want to see me?" she cooed, as she gave him a wicked smile. "Am I in some sort of trouble?"

"Trouble, you are the meaning of trouble," he shouted, as he took a few steps closer to her. "Do you realize what you have done? Plans were in motion to attack Evergreen tomorrow. By retrieving Thomas, you have put them on alert."

"I know it was foolish," she yawned. "But, I wanted him. You said that I could have him. He is my brother after all. I have always wanted to play with a brother."

"How did you do it?" Jario asked, as he began to pace back and forth in front of her. "Did anyone see you?"

"No one saw me. No one at all," she smiled and tugged on the bottom her corset to reveal more of the top of her breasts. "No one saw me, because, I looked like my sister. I looked exactly like Lady Lara."

"How?" Jario stood in shock. "When were you given the power to change your appearance?"

"I found that I received it through your blood," she smirked, as she licked her finger remembering his rich blood upon her tongue. "The night you showed me how you could change your body, I drank your blood. I always drink your blood when you bed me. I received your power through it, and I didn't have to suffer with scars, burns, or blisters."

"You had no right to take my power. You had no right to use the power," Jario screamed. "It was given to me. It was mine to use. I shared it with you to fuel your desires and to make you scream your undoing."

"I thank you for that amazing evening," she smirked, as she ran her tongue over her lips and smiled. "It was delightful. I would love to do it again, but I have someone new to entertain my fantasies."

"I am warning you, Magna," Jario screamed, through his gritted teeth. "If the army fails to destroy Evergreen and I am unable to retrieve Lady Lara, I will have your head."

He turned and stormed out of the Grand Hall in search of Buck. Magna watched him leave and stepped back upon her stool.

"Bolivia," she called, to her dressmaker. "Dear, you can come back and finish my dress. The mean vampire is gone."

Chapter 21

They had been gone for what seemed like forever. Lady Lara sat trying to control the pain in her body, and the fear of what her sister, Magna, had done. Seeing several people move from the doorway to clear a path, Elda entered the Command Center with Baxter and Oliver following close behind. Standing to see beyond Oliver for   any sign of Thomas, she only saw the slump of Oliver's shoulders and his eyes staring at the floor.

"Where is Thomas?" Lara asked, as she grabbed Oliver's bulky arms to keep from falling. "Why has he not returned?" Searching his eyes for answers, Lara saw the sadness in his eyes. "Tell me what has happened to Thomas."

"My Lady, he was not in the stable," Oliver whispered, as he gently moved her back toward the bench. Helping her sit, he knelt down before her and covered her trembling hands within his own. "Magna has taken him. I saw the red wisp of smoke."

Tears began to fall from Lady Lara's eyes. Pulling her hands from Oliver's, she stood with resolve and straightened her back. Watching the people she loved gather around her, she stepped forward to address them.

"Lord Thomas has been taken by an enemy of Evergreen, my evil sister, Magna," Lara tried to remain calm as she spoke to her people. "I can only assume that he is being held at Black Thistle Castle. With Jario's army preparing to attack, Lord Thomas would want us to be strong and defend Evergreen. I have sent word to Cumberland Castle of Jario's attack upon Baxter and the information Gavenia so bravely received.

They will arrive at sunset tomorrow to fight by our side. It is late. Please take your leave and rest. A war is coming that I intend to win. When we have won and Thomas is brought home, I will have the pleasure of taking the heads of the traitor, Jario, and my sister."

Loud cheers filled the chamber as Lady Lara walked through the crowd looking at the faces of her faithful people. Making her way toward the doorway she stopped, turned toward the room, and offered a deep curtsy to everyone. Lady Lara left quickly before she fell apart in front of everyone. Elda followed closely behind her.

Stepping from the room, she stopped to lean against the stone wall. Closing her eyes, she reached out for Thomas' mind. Weaving her way through the darkness and then a heavy thick blanket of fog, she found him. He was sleeping. He was dreaming of their first kiss.

Taking Elda's hand and squeezing it tightly, she whispered with relief, "He is sleeping. I dare not wake him."

"My Lady, is he at Black Thistle Castle?" Elda asked.

"I could not tell. He was not awake," she replied. "I will try later, but first we need to see Meadow. Come, let's hurry."

Lady Lara and Elda sped through the hallways to the stone steps of the tower that led to Meadow's chamber. Reaching the witch's door, it swung open before they could knock as Elda took her place outside Meadow's door.

"Come in," Meadow waved her hand for her seat herself, as she closed the door with a snap of her fingers. "I am sorry that Thomas has been taken."

"Thank you. Do you know where my sister has taken him?" Lara asked, knowing the answer she would receive.

"I need not tell you for you already know," Meadow replied, as she took a sip of her clover tea. Placing the cup on the saucer, Lara watched as it drifted through the air and lightly sat upon the table next to her. "However, this is not what you have come to ask of me. Your pain has troubled you for some time. I believe that you know what causes it."

"I had hoped, but I was not sure of it," Lara responded, as she placed her hands upon her stomach. "Had we not had the news of Jario's attack, I would have come sooner."

"It is what you believe," Meadow whispered, as she smiled and placed her finger against her lips.

Closing her eyes, Lara saw her lips move but heard no sound. Meadow opened her eyes and flicked her finger toward a candle that sat on the wooden beam above the hearth. The candle burst into a rose colored flame.

"It is a female child," Meadow softly said. "Take great care to hide her from Jario. If he knows of her, he will threaten harm to her to force you to leave Thomas and take him as your mate."

Lara brought her hand to her mouth and gasped, "It is true? I am with child?"

"Yes, it is true," Meadow replied. "Keep her safe and Evergreen's people will thrive. This is all I have seen. I can tell you no more."

Lara stood and placed her hands against her stomach. Turning to leave, she watched the door swing open before her. As she stepped through the doorway, Elda took Lady Lara's hand to steady her.

"Good evening," Meadow said, before she blew out the candle upon the wooden beam and her hand beckoned her teacup.

"Good evening," Lara replied. "Thank you. I will find a way to protect her."

* * *

Back in her room, Lara sat upon the edge of their bed. The joy she felt for the child she was carrying was overshadowed by the abduction of Thomas. She knew she could keep the child safe within the castle, but it would become their prison, if Jario could not be dealt with quickly. She fell back against the bed linens and tried to calm her fears. Turning her head toward Thomas' pillow, she inhaled his scent and let it fill her mind with the love they shared.

Reaching again for him with her mind, she worked her way through the darkness until she found him sitting on the floor of a damp cell. He peered through the bars at the light offered by the torches. His sight was blurry, but not from spells or potions. He was in need of blood.

"Thomas, can you hear me?" Lara whispered, through their connection into his mind. "If you can, do not allow anyone to discover it. Try to answer me in your mind." She saw Thomas' eyes flutter and realized he had heard her. "Good, I know you heard me. Are you well?" She waited for his response and saw him nod his head. "Are you alone?" He nodded again. "We will get you out of there, my love. Be strong for me. I love you above all others, for all eternity." She could read his love for her in his mind and wanted to hold him next to her. "We will save you, Thomas. You will be home soon." His eyes closed, and she lost their connection.

* * *

The sound of slippers upon the stone floor woke Thomas. He knew that someone was there, but he could not see anyone. He had tried to use his vision, but it had failed him. He was too weak for his gift to help him.

"Brother," Magna chirped, as she walked toward the cell and stood resting her hands upon her knees. Exposing the tops of her breasts, she waited for Thomas' eyes to look at her. When he did, she saw the glazed appearance of his eyes. "What has happened to your eyes?"

"I am blind," Thomas replied, as he tried to stand. "I made a bad bargain with the old witch, Velsa, and my payment was my sight."

"I hate Velsa," Magna said, as she examined his eyes as he moved closer to her. "You cannot heal yourself?"

"No, I am unable to heal my eyes," he replied, in a low and controlled tone of voice. Trying to lift his arms to grab the bars, he gave up feeling them too heavy.

She watched as he pressed his face against the bars. "Your eyes are pale and cloudy. I had hoped to show you my new dress. I had it made especially for this occasion."

Stepping back, she twirled around to show off her new attire.

"I am sure it is lovely," Thomas replied, hearing the rustle of the fabric. "Could you tell me the color? I can try and picture it in my mind."

Enamored, Magna stepped closer to the bars. She lifted her hand and stroked the side of Thomas' face. "It is red with black lace at the shoulders. The skirt is full."

"It sounds beautiful," Thomas said, trying to keep Magna calm. He had heard stories of her fits of anger and wanted no part of them. "I wish I could see it."

Tilting her head, she was confused by his lack of fear. For now, she was enjoying the pleasant conversation. There was time enough for blood and pain. His blindness was a problem she wanted to fix. If he couldn't see the blood and her naked body, the games would not be as much fun.

"Are you in need of blood?" she asked, as she studied him closely. She watched him try once more to lift his arms. "Do you feel the madness grasping for you?"

"I am in need of blood," Thomas replied, as he wiped his mouth with his hand. "It has been too long. I was careless and have not taken blood for a while."

Magna tore her wrist with her fangs and placed her arm through the bars. He stepped back trying not to show that he was sickened by her offer.

"It is my blood or blood of a human," she growled. Placing her other hand upon her waist as she tapped her foot impatiently. "I have nothing else to offer you."

Not wanting to consume human blood, he reached for her arm. His hands found her hand, and he pulled her wrist to his mouth. He could hear her moan as he pulled the sour blood into his mouth and swallowed until she pulled her arm away.

"Rest, I must go," she said, as she stepped back from his cell. I want to watch the army leave for Evergreen. If they are lucky, my sister will occupy the cell next to yours very soon. I will be back later."

Thomas backed away from the bars. Hearing her leave, he tried to concentrate on Lara. He needed to warn her. The army was on their way. He strained and pushed with all the effort he could muster. Suddenly, Lara answered him.

"I hear you," Lara said, knowing something was wrong. "What has happened?"

"The army is leaving to attack Evergreen," Thomas replied. "Magna told me she was going to watch them leave. Warn Preston and Tate."

"I will," she gasped, as she thought of the harm that could come to her people. "Has she harmed you?"

"No, she has not harmed me yet. I will do what is necessary to survive," Thomas responded. "Know that I love only you. Anything I do is to be able to return to you."

"I understand, my love," Lara replied, as she realized he was in the clutches of her evil sister. Blood, torture, and pain was the reward for refusing her advances. "I will leave you to warn the others. Stay safe, my love."

"And you, sweetheart," Thomas replied. Tears fell upon his cheeks as he let go of their connection.

Chapter 22

The army began to gather in the courtyard under Jario's balcony. The smallest men adjusted their breastplates and leather quivers full of arrows over their backs. As the smallest men, they carried the lightest weapons and were expected to run the tunnels and hide in the Evergreen Forest until the signal was given. A few other men were readying the horses to pull the wooden carts loaded with axes, heavy chains baring clusters of spikes, and wooden torches wrapped in cloth that had been soaked in animal fat.

Hearing the doors to Jario's balcony open, the men scurried into formation and stood quietly at attention. Jario placed his hands wide upon the balcony wall and peered down upon his army. He could see their anxious faces and realized that not all of them would survive the attack on Evergreen. Since Magna had ruined his plans and kidnapped Lord Thomas, he knew he had to attack tonight. Otherwise, he would be in the position of trying to defend his own castle.

"My faithful army," Jario shouted, so that everyone would be sure to hear him. "It is time to bring Evergreen to their knees. Three commands will attack Evergreen, tonight. Buck will lead the command that will attack from the cliffs. Gusty will lead the wagons and men on horseback. Drake and Charlie will lead the command that will run the tunnels. It will be a fierce battle, and a battle that will bring death to some of you. Defend the man that stands next to you with your life. Be brave and bring honor to Black Thistle Castle with the destruction of our enemy, Evergreen Castle. Under no circumstances is harm to come to Lady Lara. The man, that returns her safely to me, will be given great privilege within this castle. Now, go! Bring back a victory!"

The men cheered raising their fists in the air. Running toward their assigned commands, the men calmly marched through the gate towards war. The wagons moaned from the weight of their heavy loads as they moved across the drawbridge. Jario stood on the balcony and watched his army until he could no longer see them. Satisfied that he would have his victory, he stopped for a moment to gaze at the moon before the clouds took the night's brightness away. Stepping back into his chamber, he was greeted by Magna's scent of smoldering coals before he saw her.

"What are you doing here?" Jario demanded, as he strode past her and claimed a chair by the empty hearth. He raised his chin and glared at Magna as she moved to stand before him. "You are no longer welcome in my chamber. Have you forgotten? I am the master of this castle, and you show me little regard."

Ignoring his rampage, Magna rolled her eyes and stepped toward Jario.

"Do you know that Thomas is blind?" Magna asked, as she stood before Jario. "He made a very bad bargain with Velsa. She took his eyesight." Magna stepped around his chair. Raking her fingers across his shoulders, she could feel his instant arousal. "I want to play a game with him, and I need his blindness healed."

"I knew he was blind, but I did not know the cause," Jario said, as he swatted at her hand trying to control his need for her. "You want to play games with him? What kind of games?"

"I want to change my appearance," she said, waiting for Jario's reaction. Seeing no noticeable sign of irritation, she continued. "I want to change my appearance . . . so that . . . I look like my sister."

"You have already done so," Jario sneered, as he stood and turned his back to her. "You will do it even if I tell you not to do it."

"I want to look like my sister, and I want you to act as my lover in front of him," she smirked, noticing a glimmer of approval as his shoulders twitched. "I want to fool him. I want him to think my sister has decided to be your mate, to save him. It will drive him mad. Once he is mad, I will play the games I like to play until he screams."

"That is a game I would enjoy playing," Jario snickered, as he turned and stepped toward her taking her arms within his hands. Looking into her eyes, he grinned. "I will speak to Gautier. I am sure he can create a spell to counter Velsa's."

Magna clapped her hands with glee and dashed to the door. As she stood before the door, she gazed back at Jario. Giving him a wink, she vanished into a wisp of red smoke.

* * *

Thomas looked up when he heard the boots that belonged to the voice he had heard earlier. The closer they moved to the cell door, the louder they became. A whisper of words he did not understand floated about his head. He could feel his face warm and his eyes began to sting. Fearing to stand, he pressed his back against the stone wall to steady himself. The stinging continued, and he could feel moisture forming in his eyes. Squinting his eyes as tightly as he could, he saw a bright flash of light behind his eyes and felt them begin to throb.

"Open your eyes," the voice demanded. "Show me your eyes."

Thomas pushed himself up the wall with his hands. Keeping his eyes closed, he moved forward until his hands reached the bars of the cell. Feeling the stinging and throbbing slowly subside, he tried to open his eyes. The light from the torches was too bright, and he instantly closed them.

"The torches are much too bright; they hurt my eyes," Thomas said. Bringing his hand to his forehead, he tried to shield his eyes from the bright light. Trying once more, he found it too bright to keep them open. He closed his eyes again and lowered his head. "I am use to the darkness. It hurts to open my eyes."

Thomas felt a rush of air pass before his head, and the torches sizzle as they gave way to the darkness. Lifting his head, he slowly opened his eyes. Blinking his eyes several times, he was able to see the blurred figure moving toward his cell. Trying hard to focus, he felt his eyes water. Blinking again, he rubbed the water from his eyes, and he was finally able to focus upon the stranger that stood before him.

"Can you see?" the stranger asked.

"Yes. How is this possible?" Thomas asked, as he looked at the stranger before him. "Thank you for your kindness."

"You may not find this to be kind," the stranger responded. "Magna does nothing out of kindness. She would pet a lamb, only to have it for dinner. I warn you to be careful."

"I know of her evil ways," Thomas responded. "She is my mate's sister, but I will be cautious. I thank you for the warning."

"I must leave you now," the stranger replied, as he headed for the stone steps.

"Sir, has the army left for Evergreen?" Thomas asked, with worry in his voice.

"Yes, they have started their journey to attack Evergreen," he replied. "There will be a war before the sun rises. Jario believes that he will win and gain Lady Lara as his reward. I believe that he will fail. His army is outnumbered and lacks the skills to fight a war. He is also foolish. He has sent everyone away from the castle to fight and left no one to protect his castle." Appearing to hear something in the distance, he hurried up the dungeon steps, and he was gone.

Thomas stood with his hands upon the bars of his cell. It had been some time since he had seen his own hands. He was overwhelmed by the stranger's kindness, but was suspicious of why Magna had seen fit to help him. He would worry about her when the time came. For now, he would use his eyesight to help him figure out a way to escape this dungeon.

Reaching for Lara with his mind, he hoped she would hear him. Just as she answered, he saw Jario escorting Lara into the dungeon. Confused, he stared at Lara. He couldn't believe his eyes. She stood directly in front of him, holding Jario's hand.

"What is this?" Thomas shouted. "Have you betrayed me with the traitor?"

"Thomas, I am not there with you, my love. I am at Evergreen. What you see is a trick to fool you," Lara said, into his mind. "I can see what you see. It is not me. It is an imposter."

Shaking his head, he stared at the sight before him.

"Did you do this Jario? Did you give me back my sight so that I could watch her in your arms? Lara, he is a traitor to your people. How could you do this?" Thomas roared, not understanding how Lara was speaking to him when she was right in front of him.

"Thomas, my love," Lara begged, for him to listen to her. "It must be a spell. I am at Evergreen Castle preparing for war. Tate and Gavenia are making a plan to rescue you."

"Jario, he is in shock," she smirked, as she ran her hand down the side of Jario's face. "He does not understand that I am doing this to save him." She turned and winked at Jario. "As we agreed, I am willingly giving myself to you so that he may be saved. You promised me he would be saved."

"Thomas, I have made a bargain with your mate to become mine," Jario said, directly to Thomas. "In return, we will let you return to Evergreen. You may return after Magna has had her fill of you."

"You have betrayed me with our enemy," Thomas yelled, as he watched Jario turn Lara to begin untying her laces. He saw his hands run over her bare shoulders, as her dress began to slip from her body. Turning his face, he could not bear to look at her anymore.

"Thomas, listen to me," Lara begged, with as much love as she could send toward him. "What you see before you, is not me. I love you. I would never betray you. Jario and Magna are trying to drive you mad."

127

"Thomas, she is telling you the truth," Baxter said, as he nudged his way into Thomas' mind. "I am your trusted friend and would never lie to you. Lady Lara is here with us. She is not at the Black Thistle Castle."

"Baxter?" asked Thomas, speaking into his mind as he tried to ignore the moaning coming from Lara, as Jario ran his hands down her bare back. "Is that really you?"

"Yes, My Lord," Baxter said. "It is your friend. I am here keeping Lady Lara safe. Play along with them. Magna must have taken Lady Lara's form. Do not let them know you can contact us."

"I will try," Thomas said. "It is very hard to watch him put his hands on her, even though she is not Lara."

"I know," Lara replied. "My love, be strong for me."

"The stranger told me all of the army has left Jario's castle," Thomas said, as he looked again at Jario pressing his body against the imposter."

"If this is true, I will send Tate to help you escape," Baxter replied.

"Be careful," Thomas responded, as he lowered his head to avoid looking at the tangled naked bodies upon the stone floor. "I must not let them suspect I am speaking to you. I will go."

"We will come for you soon," Baxter said.

With those words, Lara and Baxter left his mind. He was, once again, faced with watching the imposter wither under Jario's mouth.

"Stop, I cannot take any more of this," Thomas yelled, as he tried to laugh inside of his mind to keep himself sane. "You have dishonored me. I release you from our bond. Please stop, you are driving me mad."

The imposter turned her head and faced Thomas, giving him a broad smile.

"I am sorry my love. I do this to protect you," she whispered, as Thomas turned his back on her and leaned his head into the corner of the cell.

Chapter 23

After hearing about the warning from Thomas, Will and Frances raced with two groups of men to hide among the tops of the trees. Oliver led a group to the walls of the castle that overlooked the cliffs. Woodward took Charlotte, along with the human women, to the underground rooms behind the hidden doors. He took a moment to kiss her forehead before closing the doors and then ran to join the men above the castle. Armed with his crossbow, he took his place at the wall and waited for the attack. They all watched as the message falcon flew towards Cumberland Castle to advise them of the imminent attack, but it was feared they would be unable to arrive in time.

Lady Lara stood in the Council Chamber listening to Preston's plan to defeat Jario's army. Her thoughts kept drifting to Thomas. He had been told by the stranger that Black Thistle Castle was unprotected. If this information could be trusted, it would be their best chance to retrieve Thomas.

"I want to try and retrieve Thomas," Lara interrupted Preston. "He was told that the castle is unprotected. This is our best chance to save him."

"My Lady, we need everyone to protect Evergreen," Preston tried to persuade her to focus on the attack. "We can take out the enemy and then head toward Black Thistle Castle. We will have the numbers to surround his castle, and Jario will have to surrender or face a final death."

"If you won't help me, I will go by myself," Lara argued. "Thomas lost his eyesight to find me and bring me home. I can do no less for him."

"My Lady, no! It is too dangerous for you," Preston said, as he looked to Tate and Elda for support. "If Jario should capture you, Evergreen would be lost. Think of your people and what it would mean if that happened."

"My Lady, listen to him," Baxter said, as he looked at her hoping to change her mind. "You saved me. Without you, I would have been lost. How many others have you saved? If something happens to you, our world will change. You are the light that keeps the goodness in our souls."

"Sweet Baxter," Lara smiled, as she gently touched the side of his face. "I love you all, but I love Thomas above all others. Everything I am now is because of his love for me. Without him, I have nothing. Without him, I will cease to exist." Pausing for a moment, she glanced at Gavenia. She knew she understood her words more than anyone. "Again, I will go by myself."

"I will take you," announced Tate, as he reached for Lady Lara's hand. "I will protect you with my life."

"If Tate goes, I go too," Gavenia smiled, as she slipped her hand into Tate's. "My hawk may be of use to you. I can watch from above."

Elda nodded at Baxter. "If you are going, Elda and I cannot stay behind and miss all the fun," Baxter laughed. "When do we leave?"

"If you are determined to do this, you must leave before the attack starts," Preston sighed, fearing the harm that would come to Lady Lara. "To reach the cliffs, Jario's army will have to go through the village to avoid being seen. Since the army is made up of a majority of humans, they will be slow moving unless they are on horseback. The main attack will come from the forest. If they are underground in the tunnels, it should be safe to go through the forest if you hurry."

"I can move them quickly," Tate responded. "I can have them to the far edge of the forest before the men make their way through the tunnels. The tunnels will be more dangerous with more people scraping against the walls. They will have to go slow to avoid the tunnels collapsing."

"If you are sure," Preston looked at Lady Lara before looking at everyone else and seeing them nod in agreement. "Get your weapons and be off with you. Bring home Lord Thomas."

The small group scurried from the room to prepare for their quest.

* * *

Complete silence and the darkness had allowed Thomas to relax. Jario and the imposter had finally left the dungeon. Knowing how wicked Magna had been in the past, he determined that she must have arranged that performance. He was relieved that he had heard Lara's words in his mind, or he would have completely gone mad. Opening and closing his eyes to make sure his eyesight had not left him, Thomas tried to be grateful for his capture. After all, it had afforded him his eyesight. Leaning back against the damp stone wall, he started to visualize in his mind all the times he had held Lara in his arms.

Before he could drift off to sleep, Magna's skirt could be heard rubbing against the rough walls as she descended the stone steps to the dungeon. As she slipped a torch into the iron bracket, Thomas could see her approaching his cell. She held a dagger in her hand and began to drag it against the bars.

"I need blood," Magna smirked, pulling a key from deep between her breasts. Unlocking the cell door, the door scraped sharply against the stone floor as she pulled it open. "Do not fight me, brother. I will be quick to offer you pain." She carefully watched as Thomas stood. He was much taller than her, and she had to tilt her head back to look into his eyes. "I see Gautier has healed your eyes." Pointing her finger at him and then at herself, she grinned. "You can thank me for this little gift. Now, you can give me something I need." She flicked her wrist and Thomas' arms were, suddenly, slammed against the cell wall. Another flick of her wrist and his feet were spread apart, firmly in place. "Do you think my sister will mind sharing? She use to share when we were children." Magna became more agitated and paced back and forth in front of Thomas. Tossing the dagger from one hand to the other, she carefully watched him out of the corner of her eye. "She loved me once. I loved her once. It is sad. Don't you think? We have not been close for a long time." Stopping her pacing, she stood directly in front of him. Pointing the dagger at his face, she rambled on without making any sense. "Did you know she wants my final death?" Magna placed her hand upon his chest. Running it down the smooth fabric of his tunic, she could feel his muscles tighten. Grabbing the hem of his tunic, she ripped it from his body and gazed at his body. "My, you are handsome."

Placing the sharp point of the blade against his chest, she waited for the soft intake of breath that always preceded the pain. Hearing the slightest gasp, she drew the dagger down his chest and watched the crimson liquid cover the edge of the blade. Thomas suffered through the pain without making a sound. Wiping the blade across her tongue, her body screamed for more of the rich liquid, as she watched the open wound heal quickly. Leaning the side of her face against his abdomen, she inhaled his earthy scent before she descended her fangs and sank them into his side. As her claws extended from her fingers, she dropped the dagger and held him tightly with both hands. Feeling them penetrate his back, his body jerked from the pain of the venom. Pressing his lips tightly together to keep from screaming, he closed his eyes hoping the pain would end.

Drawing his blood into her mouth and over her tongue, she felt the heat of his blood race through her body causing her legs to buckle. As she fell, her fangs ripped his flesh as they released. Leaning against his leg, she let the euphoric sensation consume her.

"I have a lucky sister," Magna said, as she tried to stand and felt her body continue to tremble. "I am surprised she lets you leave her bedchamber."

Thomas felt sick from the assault of her mouth against his body, but he smiled anyway.

"I am the lucky one," Thomas replied. "I have known the love of one sister and the kindness of another. I thank you for returning my eyesight." His body shivered as he began to heal from the poison of her claws. He wanted to grasp her by the neck and rip her head from her shoulders. Trying to calm her, he remembered her dress. "Where is the red dress you wanted to show me?"

Still feeling the flutter within her blood, she steadied herself and brushed her hands against her skirt as she backed away from him. Flicking her wrist, his body relaxed. He shook his hands to move the cuffs away from the raw flesh that had formed under the rough metal. Stepping from the cell, she closed the door and pulled the key from her breasts to lock the door.

"I shall go to my chamber and retrieve my dress," she laughed, as she hurried to her chamber.

Seeing the dagger upon the floor, he kicked it under the small pile of straw in the corner of the cell. If she did not remember dropping it, it would be useful when they came to rescue him.

Magna stripped off her clothes and ran her fingers over the soft fabric of the new red dress. Picking up the dress, she stepped into its opening and pulled it up over her legs and hips. Placing her hand against the bodice of her dress, she turned and stepped from her chamber into the dungeon. Looking up, she saw Thomas standing at the cell door waiting for her. Moving quickly toward him and seeing him smile, she turned her back to him.

"Will you lace me up?" Magna asked, looking over her shoulder at him. "The laces are like the laces on your breeches."

Thomas reached through the bars and fumbled with the delicate laces. Her back and shoulders were bare, and the laces started just below her bare bottom. He could hear her moan every time he accidently touched her skin. Finally securing the laces with a knot, he dropped his hands and backed from the bars.

"My fingers are too large for these tiny ribbons," Thomas attempted a laugh. Once finished, he watched her turn in circles holding her skirt out on each side. "It is lovely."

"I knew that you would like it," she responded, coming close to the cell and reaching for his arms. "I want to kiss you. Will you let me kiss you, brother?"

Thomas cringed inside and stepped toward the bars. He bent down and turned his cheek to her face. He felt her hands turn his head and her moistened lips upon his mouth. It was vile, and he hated that she had replaced the last kiss that Lara had given him with one so vulgar.

As she stepped back, Thomas forced himself to smile. He saw Magna close her eyes as if she were reliving the kiss over and over in her mind.

Remove these cuffs from me, you bitch. I will let you feel my mouth upon your throat, as I rip your head off.

Feeling his back stiffen, he stepped away from the bars. He continued to watch her dance about the room. One moment she was wicked and brazen; the next moment, she was a young child starving for attention. He preferred the young child. She seldom played with knives.

* * *

The first screams of war and death were heard just as the sky began to lighten. Jario's army was unprepared for the strength of the army that had surrounded them. Men fell to their death upon the sharp stakes hidden within the deep pits. Arrows had found their mark and left men scattered upon the soft green moss turning it red with their blood. The rough crags of the cliffs had taken many from a careless hold before axes and swords took the heads of the small group that survived the climb. The new vampires were easily captured. Once they saw the first few men fall from bleeding wounds, they lost sight of their goal and stopped to feast upon their fellow comrades.

The men had easily been collected as they climbed from the tunnel and were secured to trees until they could be brought to the cells at Evergreen. Those that refused to leave the tunnel were attacked with flaming arrows until they all surrendered and climbed up from the damp earth. Twenty men in all were taken from the tunnel.

Once the wagons arrived, the men jumped squarely into the fight. They barely had time to draw their swords before they were faced with Evergreen's arrows. Those that managed to escape and maneuver through the brush to join their comrades, heard the sound of singing swords and whistling arrows greeting their heads. Gusty fought valiantly to protect his men, but at the end of all of it, he lay among the dead and wounded. He had taken a blade to the shoulder and one that severed his left leg just below the knee. The final blow to his head sent him deep into the darkness.

The castle was never breeched and most of the dead were found well beyond the view of the castle. More time had been spent retrieving the dead than fighting the war. Flora and Niobe mended several wounds received by blades or axes, but none were life threatening for humans or vampires. Preston's strategy for defending Evergreen had been the reason they had all survived.

* * *

Knowing the damage that was befalling Jario's army, Buck left the cliffs and made his way to the harbor. He knew the strength of the Evergreen Army and wanted to be close to the water when the attack failed. A ship would be sailing in the early morning, and he would be its first passenger. Deciding to leave weeks earlier, he had hidden a large bundle of clothes, coins and weapons within the boulders, seldom dampened by the waves. Grabbing the bundle, he ran to the ramp and made his way aboard the tall ship. Leaning against his cabin door, he felt the long awaited pleasure of his freedom.

Chapter 24

Tate, Lady Lara and Elda stood at the edge of the Evergreen Forest looking over the meadow of wildflowers. Taking a moment to make sure that Elda had Lady Lara well hidden, Tate returned for Baxter. He had hidden himself within a large cluster of prickly holly. When Tate appeared, Baxter fought to extract himself from its clutches. Covered in scratches, he held up his hand when he saw Tate's grin. Grasping hold of Tate's arm, Baxter barely felt his feet leave the ground and the pressure of the air against his face before he was standing firmly upon the ground by the others.

"Now, that was much easier than being carried over Oliver's back," Baxter laughed, as he slapped Tate on the back. "Thanks, my brother."

Gavenia flew overhead to scout the area. Finding the courtyard and the training area empty, she flew back to give Tate the signal. Seeing the hawk coming toward them tilting her wings back and forth, he knew it was time to proceed to the castle.

"Baxter and I learned the hard way, we cannot walk through the poison thistles," Tate told Lady Lara and Elda. "I will have to carry you. Before I do, I am going to try to enter the castle. We saw a protective spell around the castle when we were last here. If it is still up, we will have to figure out another way to enter its walls."

Tate leapt to the outer wall around the castle. Placing his hands upon the large stones, he pushed forward with his hands and watched them vanish up to his elbows. Grinning, he pulled them back, feeling relief wash over his body. Satisfied, he leapt back to the others.

"We are good. I am going to take each of you to the barracks behind the castle," Tate explained. "Gavenia found Jario's chamber near the front courtyard. This way we won't risk him seeing us. It has been a while since I was in the dungeon, and Gavenia has not found her way that deep into the castle. Let me try to find it before we all get lost or run into someone."

Agreeing with his plan, they followed Tate along the wall far away from Jario's balcony. Taking them over the wall, one at a time, they found themselves standing within the walls of Jario's Black Thistle Castle. Baxter moved Lady Lara and Elda to the shadows while Tate stepped through the stone wall in search of the dungeon.

It seemed like Tate had been gone too long, and Lara was becoming nervous. Closing her eyes, she searched for Thomas' mind. The path was dim, but easier to find. She knew immediately when Thomas realized she had entered his mind. He moved his head to give her a complete view of the dungeon.

"We are here, my love. Tate is looking for you," Lara said, as she continued to watch the view of the dungeon through Thomas' eyes.

"I am alone," Thomas replied. "Magna left the dungeon, and she has not been gone long. I am restrained with cuffs." He raised his hands carefully to show her. "Magna dropped a dagger in my cell, and I have it hidden under some straw."

"I will not ask how that happened," Lara grimaced. "Have you seen the warlock or the wolf?"

"No, I have not seen them. I have not seen the stranger either; he has not been back to the dungeon since giving me my sight," Thomas replied. "I believe that he is tired of Jario and Magna. He may be an ally. Wait a moment, I hear someone coming."

Magna stepped into the dungeon and went directly to her chamber and closed the door.

"Did you see her?" Thomas sighed. He was glad she had not come to his cell, again. He had had enough of her games.

"Yes, I saw her," Lara replied, as her voice began to quiver. "It has been some time since I have seen my sister."

Looking up, Thomas saw a brief glimpse of Tate on the stone steps and then he was gone.

"I just saw Tate," Thomas tried to keep from standing and drawing attention to himself. "Why did he not come for me?"

"If he is caught, we will not be able to find you," Lara answered him, trying to keep him calm. "He will need one of us to help him defend against Magna or Jario, if they should try and stop your escape."

"Tell me you are not coming down to the dungeon," Thomas angrily replied. "It is not safe for you to be here. Who is with you?"

"Baxter and Elda are here with me," Lara smiled, as she answered. "I am not afraid, my love. I have gifts that can protect me. Sit tight, we will be there soon." She dropped her connection before he had a chance to argue with her.

Tate led Lady Lara, followed closely behind by Baxter and Elda. As they crept along the dark hallway, they kept their bodies as close to the walls as possible. Stopping occasionally, they listened for anyone coming in their direction. Finally reaching the top of the stone steps that led to the dungeon, Lara closed her eyes and said a silent prayer to keep them safe.

They slowly descended the steps, only stopping to listen for Magna or Jario. Tate could see the shadows dance upon the wall from the torch that glowed brightly within the iron bracket. Seeing Thomas, Tate moved as quietly as he could across the stone floor to Thomas' cell. Lady Lara was the next to move. Hearing Magna humming an old childhood song, she hesitated until Tate drew her attention, and she hurried to his side. Seeing Thomas, she brought her finger to her mouth and silently signaled him to be quiet. Elda moved to the wall beside Magna's chamber, and Baxter moved back up the stone steps.

"Thomas, give me your hands," Lara said, as she beckoned him to move toward her.

He carefully held the chains against his body as he moved toward Lara. Wanting to touch her, he reached toward her face forgetting about the chains. They fell to the floor with a heavy thud. Standing perfectly still, everyone waited for Magna to exit her chamber and find them. After a few moments of silence, Lara carefully reached her hands between the cell bars and took hold of one of the cuffs. Closing her eyes, she concentrated on the metal cuff. Tate and Thomas watched as the cuff and chains turned to cloth. Smiling, she took his other hand and rid him of the remaining heavy cuff.

"How did you do that?" Tate and Thomas asked, at the same time.

"Not now, we need to get out of here," Lara whispered, as she brushed Thomas' face with her fingers. "Tate, get him out of the cell. We need to hurry."

Tate stepped through the bars of the cell and pulled his dagger from his boot. Cutting the cloth cuffs, Tate tried to grab Thomas to throw him over his shoulder. Shaking his head, Thomas pulled away and moved toward the pile of straw in the corner of the cell. He bent down and uncovered a dagger before he slipped it into his boot. Surprised, Tate motioned that he needed to pick up Thomas. He bent his knees and lifted Thomas over his shoulder. Stepping through the bars, Tate set Thomas' boots back on the stone floor.

Before Thomas could kiss his mate, Baxter moved down the steps quickly hearing heavy boots off in the distance. Cupping his ear and pointing up the steps, he moved across the dungeon to blend in with the shadows. Everyone waited for what they believed to be Jario. The boots became louder until Thomas' stranger stepped into the dungeon followed by the wolf. Freezing in place, Thomas feared the worst.

"What is this?" Gautier asked, as he stared at Thomas and the intruders. "Is this the Lady Lara I have heard Jario constantly talking about?"

Lara took a step forward. Feeling Thomas grab her arm, she pulled from his grasp and continued forward to stand before Gautier.

"I am Lady Lara of Evergreen," she softly said, as she kept an eye on the wolf. "I have come to take my mate home. He has been kidnapped by my sister."

Magna burst through the door to stand face to face with Lara. Grabbing her sister's arms, she quickly pulled her into her bedchamber and slammed the door. Tate and Thomas stepped toward the door but backed away as the wolf began to snarl and move further into the room.

"Call off your wolf," Thomas shouted. "My mate is in danger. You must know Magna feels nothing for anyone but herself."

Gautier stretched out his arm and made a fist. When his hand opened, the door to Magna's chamber flew off its hinges.

Two women stumbled out of the chamber. Two women that looked exactly like Lady Lara.

"Lara, come to me," Thomas requested. "I fear for your safety. Come to me."

He saw both women moved toward him.

"I know one of you is an imposter," Thomas smiled, knowing this was meant to fool him. Looking at both of their faces, he searched for his Lara. "Magna, I was speaking to your sister in my mind when you changed your appearance. She was in my mind, when you tried to make me believe Lara had chosen Jario. I can speak to her, right now. I can ask her to do something, and she will do it. The real Lara will hear me."

Suddenly, Magna grabbed her sister and flung her arm around her neck. She pulled a small dagger from her pocket and placed it at her sister's throat.

"Let me pass, or I will give your beloved Lady Lara her final death," Magna screamed. "I will murder my sister. Let me leave this place."

Backing toward the stone steps, she tightened her arm around her sister's neck. Gautier and the wolf moved to allow her enough room to escape.

"If you take one step toward me, I will cut her throat," Magna shrieked.

"Please, Magna. Do not harm your sister," Thomas begged, as he knelt down on one knee. "Take me. Take me. I will leave with you. Please! Let Lara go."

"No! You love Lara," Magna screamed. Tears began to well in her eyes. "You would never love me. You would always love my sister."

Taking another step back toward the stone steps, Magna caught the heel of her boot on the hem of her skirt causing her to lose her balance. Her wrist jerked, and she plunged the dagger into her sister's neck. Lara screamed and tried to grab at the blade with her hand. Tumbling to the floor, Lara felt a body slam against her back and blood running over her shoulder as her vision began to fade. More screaming and shouting filled her ears. She felt strong hands grabbed her arms and pulled her across the stone floor. Looking over her shoulder, she saw the white fur of the wolf flash before her eyes. Lara watched the wolf's jaws snap Magna's neck and rip her head from her shoulders. Closing her eyes to escape the carnage before her, Lara slowly succumbed to the darkness.

* * *

Baxter and Tate guarded the open doorway to Magna's bedchamber as Thomas gently placed Lara's limp body upon Magna's bed. The blood ran from her neck, soaking quickly into the bed linens. Sitting on the bed's edge, he leaned forward and covered the wound with his mouth. Swirling his tongue through her blood and over the wound, he felt it begin to heal. Sitting up, he brought his wrist to his mouth and tore his flesh with his fangs. Seeing the blood begin to flow from his wrist, he opened Lara's mouth and let it run across her tongue. His wrist began to heal, but he tore it again, to provide her more blood.

"My love, come back to me," Thomas whispered, into her ear. "Open your eyes. Do not leave me. I will not survive without you."

Pushing the hair from her face, he waited for a flicker of her eyelashes or a soft moan that would tell him she would not leave him.

Feeling the warmth within his chest begin to fade, he shouted for his brother, "She is leaving me. We need to take her home to Evergreen. She needs Flora's help."

"The sun is rising," Tate sighed and grasped his brother's shoulder. "It is not safe for those that cannot walk in the daylight."

"I can take her back," Baxter said, as he hurried through the chamber door. "I have the gift of flashing. I can take her to the Healing Room. Flora will be able to help her."

"Take her now," Thomas said, as he stood by the bed. Lifting Lara into his arms, he gently placed her body into Baxter's outstretched arms. "Hurry, she has little time left."

Baxter nodded and held Lady Lara tightly within his arms, letting her head rest against his chest. "I will come back for you, Lord Thomas." Closing his eyes, he whispered a few words and vanished leaving the scent of musk and pine needles behind.

Moving slowly into the dungeon, Thomas was drawn to the pool of blood upon the floor. Thankfully, Elda had seen fit to remove Magna's body from the dungeon.

"Where are the remains of Magna's body?" Thomas asked, looking around the dungeon.

"My Lord, I have placed her body outside. It is in an open area where the sunlight will turn her to ash."

"Stand watch over it," Thomas ordered. "I want to be sure she can never cause harm again. I want to be sure she is gone." Elda turned, and He watched her leave the dungeon.

Thomas could hear the panting of the wolf and turned to see Gautier standing by the open cell door. Stepping toward the wolf, he knelt down and looked into her bright blue eyes. Slowly, he nestled his fingers within her thick white fur and scratched her behind her ears.

"I owe you both so much," Thomas said, as he looked up at Gautier. Standing, he held out his hand to him. "Thank you for helping Lady Lara and giving me back my eyesight. You will always be welcome at Evergreen."

Gautier grabbed his outstretched hand and nodded. Tilting his head, he heard someone running in the distance. "I hear Jario running within the hallways. You should leave this place. He is crazed with the need for power. I foolishly provided him with a spell to enable him to change his appearance. Magna acquired that power through his blood. I fear he will use it for harm."

Before Thomas could reply, Baxter reappeared before him, "Are you ready, My Lord?" he asked, as he held out his hand. "Lady Lara is safe within Flora's care. She will need you when she wakes."

Taking Baxter's hand, he bid farewell to Gautier. "Come to Evergreen, we will speak more about this."

Turning toward Baxter, he watched him close his eyes. Hearing him whisper, he began to feel the dizziness he dreaded. The room swirled before him, and he slowly slipped into darkness.

* * *

Tate stepped out into the sunlight to see Elda standing watch over what remained of Magna's body. A slight breeze captured the ashes and swept them up into the air above her head. They swirled about, as if playing on the wind until they burst apart leaving nothing behind.

"Elda," Tate shouted. "Gautier heard Jario running through the hallways. I say we find the traitor."

Grinning, Elda ran toward Tate. Pulling her dagger from its sheath at her waist, she tilted her head signaling toward the front courtyard of the castle. Tate cocked his eyebrow and started to run. Following close behind Elda, they made their way to the front entrance of the castle. Entering into a grand foyer, they noticed large stone steps leading to the second floor of the castle. Making their way up the steps, Elda listened at each wooden door they passed. The castle was empty. No one had been left behind to protect their master. Finding no trace of Jario, they noticed another set of stone steps and took them two at a time until they reached the top. Approaching a large set of wooden doors, Elda could hear someone pacing back and forth across the stone floor.

"He is in there," Elda pointed to the heavy doors. "He is dangerous, Tate. He can turn you to stone with one touch. He has the gifts of smoke and haze."

"How do you want to do this?" Tate asked. "He must know that we are coming for him. He has not left for fear of the sunlight."

"Break down the doors," Elda replied, as she grabbed another dagger from her boot. "Push him toward his balcony and through the doors. The sunlight will take him for us."

Giving Tate a wink, Elda ran toward the door. With Tate by her side, they rammed their shoulders against the wooden doors and burst forward into Jario's chamber. Looking about the room, they found the balcony doors wide open, and the room was empty. Puzzled, Elda walked about the chamber looking for any place that Jario could have hidden. Tate stood at the open doorway in case Jario ran from a hiding place. Jario was gone or was hiding within his haze. Elda began to run about the room slashing her dagger through the air. No sound other than her boots could be heard within the chamber. Jario had managed to escape.

Confused and disappointed, they left the chamber for the courtyard. Once out in the open air, Tate took hold of Elda's arm. It was time to return to Evergreen. He leapt into the air, taking them away from Black Thistle Castle.

* * *

Hearing the screams, Jario ran through the dim hallways to find

Magna. The smoldering scent of Magna's blood drifted through the hallways. Feeling his fangs immediately descend, he sped toward the dungeon. Her scent began to surround him, as it drew him closer to the dungeon. He could smell too much blood in the air.

Stopping suddenly, he could sense her blood was laced with something different, something tantalizing sweet. The scent was familiar, but he could not place it. Inhaling deeply, the memory of her sweet blood slammed into him. It was Lady Lara's blood. Running toward the dungeon, he feared what he would find. Making the last turn before the dungeon steps, he could hear the growl of Gautier's wolf and several men shouting. The scent of death permeated Magna's blood. It was the scent of a final death. Recognizing Baxter's voice, he stepped back and fled to his chamber.

Pacing back and forth across his room, he tried to come up with a plan to save himself. Pulling the balcony doors open wide, he saw the morning sun spilling upon the balcony wall. Jumping back from the harmful rays, he ran to the door of his secret room. Pressing his foot upon the small stone in the floor, he watched it open. He could hear boots running toward his door when he stepped inside and pressed the stone release. He slumped against the wall to the floor, watching the door close. The dark room calmed his nerves until he heard the crash of his chamber doors. He could hear Elda and Tate within his chamber. They were searching for him.

He had failed Magna. He had left the castle unprotected. He had caused her final death. Hearing Elda and Tate leave the chamber, Jario laid down upon the stone floor of his secret room. Closing his eyes, he began to plot his next move.

I have failed, he thought. Yes, I have failed, but I will never give up until I have Lady Lara.

Chapter 25

The Cumberland Army had arrived after the war had ended. They had helped clear the dead bodies from the grounds and secure all of the prisoners in the dungeon. With Thomas never leaving Lady Lara's side in the Healing Room, Tate and Preston met with the Cumberland Commander. They offered their appreciation for their service to Evergreen and promised to defend Cumberland Castle if the need should arise.

Several days had passed since the Cumberland Army had left Evergreen, but Lady Lara had shown no signs of waking. Thomas sat by her side, day and night, holding her hand. He whispered words of love in her ear, hoping she could hear him. In the early morning when the castle was most quiet, Flora could hear soft sobbing coming from the Healing Room.

Thomas had not taken a meal since their return. The silver-gray of his eyes were beginning to show the red flecks of madness. Seeing this, Flora sent Niobe to find Tate. If Thomas could not be made to take a blood meal, he would become very dangerous and be lost to the madness.

"My Lord and brother," Tate said, placing his hand upon his brother's shoulder. "Has she shown any sign of waking?"

"No, she still sleeps," Thomas sighed. "She is very beautiful when she sleeps."

"She is, brother," Tate replied, as he sat upon the empty cot. "I have asked Charlotte to bring you a meal. You need your strength. You must stay strong for Lady Lara."

"I do not feel the need to eat," Thomas slurred, as he kept his eyes upon Lara's face. "I am beginning to lose hope. I fear she will never wake."

"I understand how you feel, brother," Tate responded, as he knelt beside his brother and tried to draw his eyes away from Lady Lara. "It was not long ago that I sat where you are now. I watched my Gavenia sleep as her body recovered. It is the same for Lady Lara. She will wake when she is healed."

"I could not help her," Thomas began to sob. Wiping the tears from his eyes, he looked at Tate and felt his brother's arms wrap around him. "I could not protect her from harm."

"She will wake," Tate whispered. "She will wake when she is healed. When she does, she will need you. She will need you to be strong. You must take care of yourself so that you can take care of her."

Nodding, Thomas realized the truth in Tate's words. They looked up to see Charlotte standing in the doorway with a tray of food. Tate pulled a stool from the corner of the room and took the tray from her, placing it before Thomas. He watched her glance at Lady Lara and could see the sadness in her eyes before she left.

"Eat up," Tate said, as he pushed a piece of bread layered with cheese and a cup of blood toward his brother. Lifting a small cloth from two small bowls, Tate grinned as he looked up at Thomas. "Bread pudding, Thomas. It is bread pudding. Charlotte makes the best bread pudding."

After drinking the blood and taking a bite of the bread layered with cheese, he watched Tate's finger gouge into the hot bread pudding scooping it up, and making it disappear into his mouth. The happiness upon Tate's face made him smile. Gouging his own fingers into the bread pudding, he then felt the smoothness of the pudding melt upon his tongue.

"Do I smell bread pudding?" Lara struggled to speak, as she raised herself up, leaning against her elbows. "Did you save any for me?"

Quickly, licking his fingers clean, Thomas grabbed Lara and held her tightly against his body for a moment before he began feathering kisses over her face.

"You have come back to me," Thomas sighed, with relief as he felt the warm sensation fill his body. "I have missed you." Feeling her body start to tremble, he pushed her back to look into her eyes. "You need my blood." Cradling the back of her head, he placed his wrist to Lara's mouth. He could feel her fangs sink into his wrist and the pleasure it brought him, as she drew his blood. "My love, take all that you need. Take all that you need."

Feeling satisfied she had taken enough, Lara released his arm and licked the wound with her tongue making it close. She immediately reached for his face and pulled him towards her. Capturing his mouth with hers, she could taste the sweetness of bread pudding and felt the need for his touch.

"I will leave you two love birds alone," Tate laughed, as he stood and walked toward the door. "I am glad you are well, My Lady. We are glad to have you back."

Stepping into the hallway, he could hear Lady Lara scolding Thomas for not eating. Laughing to himself, he quickly sped off to find Gavenia.

* * *

The castle was quiet, except for the wind blowing through the open balcony doors and the padding of the wolf's paws through the hallways. Jario leaned against the wall of his secret chamber. He had not left it since the morning Tate and Elda searched for him. His perfect plan had been a disaster. He had listened for his army to return from their battle. Neither Gusty nor Buck had made their way back to the castle. The first real sign that his army had lost the war. He realized he had much to learn about being the master of a castle and the leader of an army. Surrounding himself with fierce loyal vampires and never leaving the castle unguarded were important to his survival. Humans were too fragile for fighting. They were worth nothing more than a warm meal or a place to stab his manhood.

Feeling the overwhelming need for blood, Jario stood and hit the stone with his hand to open the door into his chamber. He could see the moonlight streaming in through the balcony doors and was thankful the sun had set. He took off his clothes and left them in a heap on the floor. Striding naked to the balcony, he stood in the cool night air looking up at the moon as the clouds drifted over the brightness.

I have been hiding within Black Thistle Castle like the moon does among the clouds. I will not hide any longer. I will build a new army and lead them into battle. I will be a "Master" to be obeyed and feared.

Jario opened the large wooden chest and grabbed breeches and a tunic. After tying the leather laces, he reached for the tunic and tugged it over his head. Before he could sit down to pull on his boots, he heard the sound heavy boots walking toward the broken doors of his chamber. Gautier stood in the doorway with his hands upon his hips.

"I will give you until the moon is full to pack your belongings and leave this castle," Gautier sternly ordered. "I have seen the hatred you have for anyone but yourself. This castle belonged to my brother and now it belongs to me."

"I repaired the pile of rocks you left behind," Jario shouted, as he yanked on his boots. "I will not leave Black Thistle. I am the master of this castle."

"Yes, you will leave this castle," Gautier sneered, before taking a step into the chamber. "I have the power to make you leave or give you your final death. You may enjoy blowing in the wind. I dare you to challenge me. It would delight me greatly, to end your life and let you join Magna." With a smirk, Gautier left the chamber leaving Jario stunned.

* * *

Standing within the thick forest, Jario hunted for Velsa's cottage. Desperate to find her, he started shouting her name as he made his way through the thick fog. He wandered about for hours before he sensed the cottage was near. The sound of a crackling fire and the smell of smoke filled the air before the glow from her cottage windows appeared.

He hated that she hid her cottage, and he had to wander around the forest until she decided to meet with him. It pained him to come to Velsa for help. He still owed her a payment for the last favor she granted him. Standing at her door, he started to reconsider his visit. She always required a payment. They were usually difficult or time consuming. Compared to having his body set on fire, they were nothing more than annoying. Thinking of his failures to capture Lady Lara, and the demand from Gautier to leave the castle, he clenched his jaw and slammed his fist against the door.

"Come in," Velsa hollered, as the door opened. "What were you pondering? Were you considering leaving before you knocked on my door? You must be desperate."

Ducking his head to enter the cottage, Jario made his way directly to the stool in front of the hearth. Raking his fangs over his bottom lip, he tried to ignore the fire that blazed in the hearth. Velsa snapped her fingers and the door slammed making the herbs that hung from the ceiling, shake. Giving him a quizzical look, she released a cackling laugh that caused him to cover his ears.

"You have a spell covering your body," Velsa laughed, as she pointed her finger at Jario. "It covers a painful payment. Was it worth it?"

"I had a plan," he replied, as he pushed her finger away from his face. "I thought it was part of a good plan. I had no idea it would damage me beyond recognition."

"You thought?" She smirked and turned her head to the side to spit into the roaring fire. "Your plan failed, and you have come to me for help. Who offered this spell?"

"Everything has failed," Jario shouted, as he jumped from his stool and began pacing the small cottage having to bend at the waist. "My army was destroyed, Thomas was rescued before I could obtain Lady Lara, and Gautier has demanded I leave the castle."

"What of Magna?" Velsa asked, trying to control herself after hearing Gautier's name. She paused for a moment and sighed. "Oh my, I read your pain. She has received her final death. This leaves you alone."

"Yes, my lovely Magna is gone," Jario groaned, as he ran his hand over his face and returned to his stool. "I need a favor. I need a castle of my own. I will not survive if I have to hide among the hollows of trees or in small caves during daylight. It must have protection, like your cottage. Can you help me?"

Seeing Velsa tap her gnarled finger against her wart covered chin, Jario waited anxiously for her answer. He watched her pull an old shawl over her lap and spit once more into the fire. Closing his eyes to avoid looking at the flames, he listened for her reply. Fearing she would decline him, he prepared himself to bolt from the cottage.

"I will help you," Velsa replied, seeing the relief upon Jario's face. "If you are prepared for the payment I request, I will help you."

Feeling his shoulders relax, he grabbed her hands without thinking. Sparks began to shoot from her fingers causing him to jerk his body backward. Falling off the stool, he looked at his hands covered in soot.

"Bring me the tail of the white wolf," Velsa snarled. "I learned of the broken binding spell, and I am not over the pain of losing Gautier to that mongrel." Seeing his concerned expression, Velsa knew he needed the castle for protection. "This will be a difficult task, and I understand it will take time. I will give you a castle. However, I give you a strong warning. If you ignore the payment, I will bind you to your new castle as I did Gautier."

"I accept," Jario stated, as he stood on trembling legs. "I accept the payment you require."

"Sit down, you make me nervous with all your moving about," she snarled. "Out of the kindness of my very old heart, I will repair your damaged body. Gautier had no need to harm you with his spell. Sit quietly and I will get to work."

Jario tried not to move. He had received all he had asked for and more. He closed his eyes as the flames within the hearth began to roar. He could hear her chanting and feel his tunic move from the air that swirled about him. Strange scents drifted toward him, and he gagged repeatedly. Feeling his body heat, the memory of burning blasted his mind. Slowly the heat left his body and Velsa's chanting stopped.

"You have your castle," Velsa announced, turning to throw the remains of her wooden bowl into the fire. Green sparks flew from the flames, and she swatted them away from her head. "Your new castle stands beyond Hunter's Point. Once you reach Hunter's Point, it is two days ride by horse. If you show them kindness, there are plenty of farms along the way to offer you a hot meal and a place out of the sun. You will recognize the Crimson Claw Castle by the three turrets that overlook the Dragon's Tear River. A black banner with a red dragon flies above the castle."

"Your payment will not be forgotten," Jario promised, as he stood and made his way to the door. "If she had two tails, I would bring them both."

"Aren't you forgetting something?" Velsa asked, standing with her hands upon her hips. "You need the phrase to hide your castle and make it appear again." She watched him stop and turn toward her. "Claim the Darkness is to be used to hide your castle. Bring the Light is to be used to make your castle appear. Do you think you can remember these words?"

"I will," Jario grinned. "I bid you good evening." Seeing the door open, he hurried through it and ran from the cottage.

Chapter 26

Gavenia stood while Niobe pulled the laces of her wedding dress. It was a simple moss green dress that reminded her of the tops of the trees and the light green fields her hawk saw from the air. The layers of sheer fabric fluttered in the breeze from the open chamber window. A crown of freshly picked flowers sat upon a wooden chair with a pair of new soft leather slippers resting upon the floor.

She had decided, with Tate's approval, to have a simple intimate ceremony among the pine trees of the forest. Tate had made a small altar covered in lichen and moss to hold the dagger, three candles, and a blue cord. Niobe had decorated the branches around the altar by hanging crystal globes filled with candles.

Picking up a delicate shawl embroidered with golden threads, Gavenia nervously wrapped it around her shoulders. Niobe stood on her tiptoes to place the crown of flowers upon Gavenia's head. The sun had finally set, and it was time to make their way to the forest.

Tate stood with Omar at the altar. Omar, the Head of the Council, wore his long robe of dark green brocade. It was his usual attire for special occasions. Tate stood with his hands behind his back. Looking down at his polished black leather boots and dark green breeches, he remembered wearing them to his brother's wedding. His cream tunic sleeves were embroidered with small golden feathers to honor Gavenia's hawk. Lady Lara stood with Flora, Elda, and Baxter. Oliver, Will, Tolin, Woodward and Preston stood together on the other side of Tate.

Seeing the horse drawn wagon approach, Tate stepped forward to meet Gavenia. Charlotte and Niobe had decorated the wagon with wildflowers. They had even laced ribbons and flowers through Mona's mane and tail. Thomas jumped from the wagon and helped Charlotte and Niobe down from the back of the wagon. Taking their places next to Lady Lara, they all smiled as Tate lifted Gavenia from the wagon. Taking her hand in his, he walked her to the altar.

"You are so lovely," he said, as he brought her fingers to his mouth to softly kiss her fingertips.

"I find you are even more handsome today," she smiled shyly.

Omar pulled a small leather book from his robe and opened it using the blue ribbon that marked the page.

He began to speak, "Today we come to witness the joining of Gavenia and Tate for all eternity. Their love for one another is strong. It has been tested and proven to be worthy. Tate, do you pledge your trust, honor, love, and protection to Gavenia forever more?"

Tate stood tall and proudly said, "I will, forever more."

Looking at Gavenia, Omar continued to speak, "Gavenia, do you pledge your trust, honor, love, and protection to Tate forever more?"

Gavenia looked deep into Tate's eyes and replied, "I will, forever more."

Omar looked up at the small gathering surrounding the couple and asked, "Do you pledge your trust, honor, love, and protection to Gavenia and Tate?"

In unison they responded, "We will, forever more!"

"As a symbol of their unity, they have decided to light a single candle," Omar announced as he moved aside letting the couple advance.

Gavenia and Tate made their way to the altar and each picked up a burning candle. "Each of their candles represents a single soul," Omar explained. "Bringing the center candle to flame symbolizes the mingling of their souls. They will be forever changed as their souls will become one."

Each placed the flame of their candle upon the wick of the center candle, bringing it to flame. Blowing out their candles, they placed them down upon the altar. Stepping back in front of Omar, Gavenia and Tate waited as he took the dagger and cord from their resting place.

"By the offering of blood to one another, they unit themselves for all eternity."

Omar pierced their wrists with the point of the dagger. Pressing their wrists together, he wrapped the blue cord around their arms joining their wrists.

"It is with great honor that I declare Gavenia and Tate united for all eternity. Tate, you may kiss your mate."

Tate bent down and kissed Gavenia to the sound of cheering and clapping echoing through the trees.

Thomas slapped Tate on the shoulder as he offered his hand, "Congratulations! May I kiss my new sister?"

Tate nodded and watched his brother kiss Gavenia gently on her cheek. Joining Thomas by his side, Lara wrapped her arms around Tate's shoulders and wished him well. His friends and members of the army offered their congratulations and each took their turn kissing Gavenia's cheek.

It had been decided by Tate and Gavenia to spend their first night together in a secret location. Since they would be away from the castle, Charlotte and Niobe had placed a basket full of food and sweet wine in the back of the wagon. Taking Gavenia's hand, Tate lifted her up into the wagon. Seating himself beside his mate, he felt her rest her hand upon his shoulder as she waved to their friends. Giving a short cluck with his tongue, Mona began their short journey from Evergreen Castle.

"Gavenia, we are on the edge of eternity," Tate whispered. "I will enjoy every moment of it."

Feeling Gavenia lean her head against his shoulder, he was the happiest he had ever been. He was anxious to arrive at the surprise he had planned for her. They both wanted a secret location for their first night, but he had decided to keep it secret, even from her. Coming to a halt, he tethered Mona and lifted Gavenia from the wagon.

"Where are you taking me?" she asked, as she looked around and saw nothing but trees.

Pulling a wide piece of ribbon from the handle of the basket, he bound her head to cover her eyes, "It is a surprise."

Taking her hand and the basket, he led her into the forest. Stepping slowly through the forest, he finally stopped and untied the ribbon. Before her, was a wooden platform built high among the trees. Looking at Tate with a puzzled look, she walked toward the ladder leaning against the edge of the platform.

"What is this?" She asked, giving him a kiss on his chin.

"You go first," Tate smiled. "I won't let you fall."

Gavenia lifted the hem of her skirt and made her way up the ladder. To her surprise, there before her was a feather mattress covered in soft linen. Candles in crystal bowls were scattered upon the floor of the platform.

"I wanted to do this for you and for your hawk," Tate smiled, as he watched her cover her mouth with her hands and gasp. "You love the feeling of flying through the trees. This is my gift to you, Gavenia. I will always love you."

Tears began to fall from Gavenia's eyes. Wrapping her arms around his waist, she placed her face against his chest.

"It is beautiful Tate. It is perfect," Gavenia whispered. "I love you, Tate."

Taking his hand in hers, she led him to their bed. It was their secret sanctuary in the trees.

* * *

Walking hand in hand back to the castle, Thomas led Lara to their private courtyard. He had a surprise waiting for her. He had asked McDuff for his help and found that he was more than willing to help him with his plan to surprise Lara. He had rimmed the fountain with candles and prepared a small table with a decanter of Lara's favorite sweet wine. Pushing the door open, Thomas watched Lara smile as she took in the flickering candlelight.

"Thomas it is beautiful," Lara sighed, as she turned and wrapped her arms around his chest. "We have not been here since you proposed to me."

"Preparing for my brother's wedding reminded me of the night you accepted me as your mate," Thomas said, as he kissed the top of her head and inhaled her fresh scent. "Have you added a new scent to your bath? The scent of ripe apples lingers on your skin."

"No," Lara looked puzzled and then remembered helping Charlotte in the kitchen. "I helped Charlotte cut apples for the food basket. The juice from the fruit must still be on my hands."

"It smells wonderful," Thomas sighed, as he lifted her hands to his mouth and kissed her fingers. "I thought we could sit under the stars and drink your favorite sweet wine before I carry you off to our chamber."

"You have thought of everything," Lara replied, as she placed her arm through his as they walked through the courtyard to the table.

After sipping the sweet wine and reminiscing about their first night together, Thomas placed a small wooden box upon the table before Lara. Seeing the gift, she brushed the back of her hand under his chin and smiled. The heat of her touch began to distract him, and he quickly tapped the top of the box. Withdrawing her hand, she picked up the box and lifted the small clasp. Lara could see a gold locket nestled within soft velvet. She ran her finger over the surface of an intricately engraved tree.

"Thomas, it is beautiful," Lara gasped, with joy. "Will you help me put it on?"

Standing, he pulled the gold locket from the box and released its clasp. Watching Lara sweep her hair from her neck, Thomas secured the clasp and kissed her neck, just behind her ear.

152

"My father gave this locket to my mother on their wedding day," he said, as he stepped around to see it rest between the fullness of her breasts. "It is all that I have to remember my mother, but I want you to have it. It brought her great joy. She would have wanted you to have it."

"Thomas, I am honored to wear this precious gift," Lara smiled and reached for his hand and drew it to her cheek. "I will wear it always. Now, take me to our chamber. I need to find a way to thank you for this lovely evening."

Before she could finish her request, Thomas lifted her up into his arms. Her laughter filled the night's sky as he feathered soft kisses upon her face.

* * *

The sun began to rise and its soft golden rays filtered down upon the bed linens that covered Tate and Gavenia. The sounds of bird's sweet morning melodies gently woke Gavenia from her dreams. Opening her eyes, she found Tate had been watching her.

"Good morning," Tate smiled and moved wisps of her red hair from her face. "How is my love this morning? Did you sleep well?"

Feeling her face blush, Gavenia looked up into Tate's eyes, "I do not believe that we slept more than a few moments."

Enjoying the rose coloring upon her cheeks, he turned toward her and rested his body upon his elbow. He drew his finger from the indentation of her throat down between her breasts, "Was it everything you hoped for?"

Gavenia placed her hand upon the side of his face and leaned forward to kiss his lips, "I remember every kiss you placed upon my lips and every touch of our bodies. The night was heavenly." She could hear a very faint sigh of what she thought was relief. "Were you disappointed?" she asked, as she lowered her eyes. "Were you disappointed that you were not the first to claim me? I was pure until . . . the dungeon."

"No, my love," Tate lifted her chin to look into her eyes. "You could never disappoint me. You and your hawk are everything to me." He looked into her eyes and rubbed his thumb against her bottom lip. "I claimed your love and your body last night, and you claimed mine. It was our first time. Our journey through eternity started last night. What happened before last night, no longer exists."

"Thank you," Gavenia said, as she wiped a tear from her eye. Feeling the warmth and security of Tate's embrace, she slowly moved to kneel between his legs, letting the bed linens fall from her body. With her arms upon his shoulders, she bent to place a kiss upon his nose. Smiling, she whispered, "I want to taste some more of Charlotte's bread pudding. I am so hungry."

Grabbing her waist with both hands, Tate could hear her sweet laugh as he flipped her beneath his body. Raising his body up, he pulled the bed linens over their heads. "You will have to wait, my love. I am famished, and only your sweetness can satisfy me."

Gavenia's sudden gasp echoed among the tops of the trees as Tate feathered kisses down between her breasts and beyond.

Chapter 27

The slamming of wooden trunks and yelling could be heard coming from Jario's bedchamber. He had made it back from Velsa's cottage before the sun began to lighten the sky. Since then, he had been packing his belongings. He had every intention of taking the gold from the hidden room, but he had found the door would no longer open. He surmised that Gautier had put a spell on it.

Hearing the soft padding of the wolf's paws, he looked up to see her sitting in the open doorway. Seeing her made him remember the payment he was required to give the old hag. He stepped closer to the wolf and felt his dagger at his hip. Her growl and the flash of her teeth made him freeze and rethink his actions.

"Off with you," Jario shouted, as he flung his hand at her. "I have no desire to see you today. I will be gone soon. Tell your master, I have a new castle. I will leave tonight." Returning to his packing, he looked back toward the doorway and saw that she had left.

Little white wolf, you will soon feel the cut of my blade when I strip you of your precious white tail.

Pulling the bed linens from the huge bed, he shoved them into a large chest with the draperies he had torn from the balcony windows. He had the doors closed to block the sun and hesitated for a moment before he opened one door. Listening for the sound of the hawk's wings, he sighed when he heard nothing but silence.

I have not seen the hawk since my army failed. Could she be wounded? I fear I have lost my hawk, and she will never find my new castle. Her absence is a sign that I must leave Black Thistle Castle.

Pacing back and forth across the chamber, he felt the anger consume his body. He thought about the fun he use to have with Buck and Gusty at the tavern. He missed them, and he missed Magna. He missed the feel of her body. He didn't miss the torture, but he missed seeing the pleasure it gave her. Her final death had been a shock to him, and he wasn't sure if he would ever get over feeling the loss. He knew that he would avenge her death one day. Thomas would face his final death by his blade. Pulling his blade from his hip, he threw it at the broken door of his chamber.

I have one more thing to do, before I leave Black Thistle Castle for good.

* * *

The flickering of light could be seen coming from under Meadow's door. Worry had filled her mind and caused her to toss and turn within her bed linens. The same dream had occurred three nights in a row. This was disturbing on its own, but the dreams delivered a warning. It was a warning she could not neglect. Along with the dream, a terrifying look into the future had presented itself to her last evening, just before readying herself for bed. She had been bent over her Book of Spells for most of the night and through morning, looking for a much needed spell. Searching the pages, she hoped to find something to help, not change, a hasty decision. She would never be allowed to change the future. As a white witch, she could only offer help. Reading page after page, Meadow studied each word and phrase.

"Here it is," she sighed with relief as she reread the spell. Feeling confident the spell would offer the needed help, she turned to calm the small books that had been flying around her chamber. "Return to your places, I need quiet." Swaying her hand from side to side, she watched as each book slowly returned to its resting place.

Gathering several items from her wooden cabinet, she precisely measured each before she poured them into the stone bowl. Drawing her finger down the spell, she made sure she had everything she needed. Lighting a white candle and placing it next to the bowl, she calmed herself and began to chant.

> Goddess of Light and Goodness hear my plea
> Protection we ask for this one in need
> Safely surround this soul for safe keeping
> Cover the mind while it is sleeping
> One is the reason a risk will be taken
> True love for all will not be forsaken

Brighten all hope with a new flame
Make eager and able ready to claim
At the end of its sound bring forth the search
Peacefully sleeping within the earth
Nearer and nearer hoping to see
A sweet scent remembered is the key
Open the binding release from the cold
Loves pure embrace reverses to old
Goddess of Light and Goodness hear our plea
Goddess of Light and Goodness we praise thee

Letting her body relax, she waved her hand and watched the flame slowly vanish. Taking a small leather pouch from the table, she poured the mixture from the bowl into the pouch. Pulling the leather bindings, she secured the spell for safe keeping. Seeing the sunlight was beginning to fade, she sat the pouch upon the table. Removing her bed clothes, she quickly put on her cream linen dress and leather slippers. Grabbing the pouch, she nodded toward the door and watched it open. Stepping through the open doorway, she hurried down the stone steps. Reaching the bottom, she snapped her fingers and heard the door to her chamber close. Satisfied, she turned and made her way through the hallway to deliver the pouch.

* * *

Sitting on the edge of the bed and looking over his shoulder, Thomas' eyes drifted over Lara's naked body. The memories of their love making filled his mind, and the scent of lemon and mint covered his body. Walking toward the window, he pulled back the heavy velvet drapes and opened the shutters. The moon was almost full, and the sky was littered with bright stars. During his blindness, he had missed so many star filled skies with Lara. Now, they would have an eternity filled with moonlight and shimmering stars.

Hearing Lara stir, Thomas turned to find her leaning back against the pillows. The locket he gave her still hung around her neck.

"My love, come back to bed," reaching her arms out for Thomas. "I have a secret to tell you."

Thomas climbed back into bed and pulled her next to his body. Kissing the top of her head, he inhaled her sweet scent and noticed the subtle scent of ripe apples still lingered in the air. As she tilted her head back to look into his eyes, his mouth took hers. The taste of her sweetness exploded against his tongue, and heat raced through his blood.

157

She was heaven in his arms, and he felt his body melt into hers.

The sound of heavy boots upon the stone hallways caused Thomas to lift his lips from her body and listen carefully. Two short strikes upon their chamber door made him jump from the bed. Pulling on his breeches before opening the door, he saw Baxter standing before him.

"What has Jario done now?" Thomas growled. "Can he reframe from trouble long enough for me to spend an evening undisturbed with my mate?"

"This time it isn't Jario, my lord," Baxter replied, with his eyes lowered to the floor after seeing Lara was still in bed. "It appears to be a band of thieves that have come to shore, looking to pillage the village. They have already burned some cottages on the outskirts of Echo Bluff. We fear they have kidnapped a young woman and taken her to their ship anchored beyond the harbor. Word has come to the army that the townspeople have seen a tall skinny man with silver gray hair. They believe him to be the leader of the vandals."

Thomas straightened and knew this must be the same man that had changed him upon the tavern road long ago. The same man that kidnapped Lara.

Was this the band of thieves that had murdered his family?

"Give me a moment, and I will meet you in the Council Chamber," Thomas shouted. "Ready a small command. We'll put an end to their foolishness and throw them in the dungeon with the remains of Jario's army."

Closing the door, Thomas made his way back to Lara. Kissing her forehead, he inhaled her sweet scent. Sitting on the edge of the bed, he pulled on his boots and tugged his tunic over his head.

"My love, I must leave you," Thomas said, as he tugged on a long strand of her hair that had fallen over her shoulder. "When I return, we will begin again, and you can tell me your secret." He stood and made his way to the door. Turning to see her face one more time before he left, he raised his hand over his chest. "I love you above all others." The door closed and he was gone.

* * *

Sitting by the warmth of the fire, Lara anxiously waited for Thomas to return. She could hardly wait to tell him her wonderful secret. A daughter would fill their future with so much happiness. Letting her mind think of soft curls and tiny hands, she suddenly remembered the warning from Meadow. Jario would stop at nothing to have her, and that could include harming their daughter.

A soft rap at the door pulled Lara from her thoughts. She opened the door to find Meadow standing before her. Stepping back, Meadow made her way into the chamber and looked about for Thomas. Seeing Lara was alone, she snapped her finger and the door closed.

"I have brought you something," Meadow said, as she opened her hand. A leather pouch sat upon her palm. "I have brought you this for protection."

"Have you seen something?" Lara gasped, as she held her hand to her throat. Taking the offering from Meadow's hand, she looked back at Meadow for an explanation. "What has happened? What have you seen?"

"You will have many decisions to make," she replied, as she folded her hands. "It is to help you and keep you safe."

"Help me do what?" Lara asked, feeling very confused. "Am I in danger?"

"I cannot say," Meadow tilted her head. "Free will cannot be tampered with. I can only offer you protection. If you should leave the castle, keep this with you. You already have protection at Evergreen, but this protects you beyond its borders."

Lara put the pouch into the pocket of her dress and offered Meadow a seat by the fire.

"Have you told Thomas of the child?" Meadow asked, as she spied a book floating across the room in her direction. Flicking her wrist and directing it back to the table, she returned her attention back to Lady Lara.

"I told him I have a secret to tell him tonight," Lara smiled with excitement. "He received news of vandals in the village, and he has gone off to secure them."

Meadow smiled as she stepped toward the door. Stopping, she returned and placed a hand upon Lady Lara's arm. "Heed my warning. Jario is a threat to the child. He will use the child against you. Keep her safe."

Making her way to the door again, she turned to see a book following her. Pointing her finger at the book, it stopped and returned to the table with a heavy plunk. With a satisfied expression, Meadow opened the door and left without a word.

Lara pulled the pouch from her pocket. Bringing it to her nose, she inhaled the pungent odor. Shaking her head from confusion, she returned it to her pocket. I need some fresh air.

* * *

Mona could hear Lara as she opened the stable door. As Lara approached the stall gate, Mona greeted her with a soft nudge of her nose. Lara rested her face against Mona's nose as she stroked the side of her face.

"I thought we might go for a ride this evening," Lara stated, as she opened the stall gate and made her way into the large stall.

She could see Arrow had been moved to his own stall next to Mona's. Reaching her hand into her pocket, she pulled out a small carrot and rested it on the palm of her hand. Arrow gently took the sweet morsel. Leaning against the wooden slats, she stood for a moment and admired his shiny black coat. Feeling Mona nudge her shoulder, she turned to see Jario standing at the stall gate.

"I am not here to harm you," Jario said, as he raised his hands to reflect his statement. "I am leaving Black Thistle Castle. It will no longer be my home."

"Should this be of concern to me?" Lara sneered, as she listened to Will wielding a sword in the Command Center and gently opened his mind. "It would be good of you to leave Evergreen and not return. You are a traitor and no longer welcome here."

"I will leave, for now" Jario offered an evil smile. "However, I will return. I will return when you least expect it. Lady Lara, you will be mine. Never forget that I want you for my own. I will not stop until you are mine."

The heavy door of the stable swung open and Will entered holding his sword. Before him, stood Jario offering a quick bow to Lady Lara. In an instant, Jario had disappeared using his haze. As Will ran forward, the sound of Jario's boots could be heard as he sped away.

Chapter 28

Lara moved swiftly through the forest without a sound. As she approached the tiny cottage, she could see a single candle flickering in the dirty window. A shadow reflecting against the seeded glass panes appeared to sway. She knew it to be the old witch moving back and forth across the room. Stepping to the door, she paused for a moment thinking of what she was about to do and why.

After the capture of Thomas and of Meadow's warning, Lara had determined this was the only way to keep her unborn child a secret and safe from Jario. Lara took a deep breath and softly rapped on the wooden door. She heard the bolt struggle and groan as it pulled from the latch. Watching the door as it swung open, it offered a view of the witch anxiously gesturing for her to come forward through the doorway. Cautiously stepping into the small cluttered room, she heard the door close, and the bolt slide back into place without assistance. Lara bent at the waist to prevent her head from hitting the ceiling that was cluttered with dried herbs and bones of all sizes. The witch was the first to speak.

"What brings you to my cottage?" Velsa asked, knowing full well what Lady Lara desired.

"I have come to bargain a favor," Lara replied. "I want to be hidden away. I am with child, and I want to protect my child from those that would do her harm."

"This requires a payment. Are you ready my dear? Are you willing to give me the payment I desire?" squawked the witch, as she twisted her gnarled hands against each other. "Once the spell is finished there is no turning back".

Lara froze with the feeling of panic and wanted to leave this place and return to Thomas, but feared for her child. Pausing for a moment, she sadly nodded her head in response.

"You must speak the words out loud my dear," said the witch, as she tilted her head waiting for Lara's reply.

Lara hesitated again for a moment more, but quietly responded by saying, "Yes, I am ready."

Seeing Lara sway slightly, the witch stepped forward taking her arm to steady her and asked, "I require a payment for this spell. I ask for the beat of your heart when your daughter reaches her sixteenth year. Since vampires do not have a heartbeat, I must make you human. Do you agree to the payment I demand?"

Lara gasped and closed her eyes. The payment the witch asked for was too high. She would forfeit all of her powers to become human. Becoming human would make her defenseless against Jario. Opening her eyes, Lara begged, "Is there no other payment that I may offer you?" Lara could feel her hands begin to tremble.

"No, I have made my demand," Velsa replied, with a smirk. "You may think on it. I am in no hurry."

Bending down, Velsa picked up a log and tossed it into the flames of the hearth. Lara watched as Velsa sat down in her chair and strummed her fingers against the wooden arms, impatiently.

Fearing she had no other option, she nodded to the witch. "Yes, I offer you the beat of my heart as payment," Lara responded, with a quiet voice as she closed her eyes hoping she was doing the right thing.

The witch flashed her toothless grin and guided her to a small bed with a gray lumpy mattress. She could see the pieces of straw and feathers protruding from holes in the covering. It smelled sour, and the bed creaked loudly as she began to lie down upon it. Lara glanced to her right, which gave her a view of the cluttered table. It was piled high with jars of dead creatures floating in colored liquid, bowls of dead mice and pottery filled with rancid smelling salves. Lara lay quietly with her hands upon her belly. Letting her mind think of Thomas and their love for one another, she could hear the witch start her chanting. The air began to crackle, and Lara could feel the heat in the air as a ball of light swirled within Velsa's hands.

Thomas, please forgive me. I only do this to protect our daughter. I will always love you.

"Bring sleep to this vampire, and her unborn child. When six full moons have passed, she will wake to walk within the sunlight. A vampire no longer, she will give birth to a human child. Keep them hidden until the child reaches sixteen years. At which time, I will collect the beat of this mother's heart as payment for this favor," chanted the old witch.

Her chanting ended as Lara wondered if she would dream of Thomas. Lara's eyelids became heavy, and she could no longer keep them open.

"Sleep now", Velsa softly murmured, as she tenderly stroked Lara's forehead. "You will be safe. A hidden cottage will be your new home."

Slowly the darkness took her and sleep was upon her.

* * *

When Thomas realized Lara was missing, he had enlisted the help of Tate, Preston, and his Evergreen army to start searching for his mate. They had tracked her to the Black Thistle Forest. There, her sweet scent of lemon and mint had vanished. The search continued through the dark damp forest until they reached the witch's cottage. Thomas could sense Velsa inside, but something else caught his attention. A hint of ripe apples lingered on the breeze. He knew that Lara's skin had held this light scent.

Suddenly, the warmth he always felt within his chest grew cold, and it was replaced with a wrenching pain. Pressing his hand against his chest, he struggled to stand and leaned against Tate to keep from falling.

Could Lara be inside the cottage under the spell of the witch, he wondered, as he hurried to the cottage door?

Placing his body against the rough wood of the door, he slammed his shoulder against it causing it to shatter as he stormed into the cottage. He franticly looked about the small room until he found Velsa calmly sitting in her rocking chair by the fire.

"Old witch, have you seen my mate?" growled Thomas, as he approached her holding his dagger. Seeing that she was ignoring him, he stepped closer to her and yelled. "Look at me."

With a smirk across her face, Velsa turned her head toward him and nodded. "I had a short visit from your fragile mate. What caused her to run? It might be good to think about her reasons for running to me," Velsa smugly said. She clucked her tongue against the roof of her mouth and leaned over the arm of her chair to spit into the fire. She slowly stood and brushed a snarled strand of hair from her face. "A lady running to an ugly witch for help is very peculiar, isn't it? Your lady requested a bargain be made, and I have held up my part," she said, as she tilted her head and looked up at Thomas' face.

Thomas could hear the old witch grinding her teeth. He watched her study his eyes and feared she would take his sight again.

"I see you have found the loophole, and you have regained your sight," Velsa smirked, as she pretended to wipe a tear from her eye. "Pity, I will miss those beautiful eyes."

Tired of her mocking tone, Thomas took a step toward the witch. As he reached for her arm, she stepped back and vanished into thin air. Nothing remained but a wisp of blue smoke. Thomas growled with rage as he picked up her chair and threw it across the room smashing everything in its path. He fell to his knees and screamed Lara's name.

"I will hunt you down, old witch," Thomas shouted. "If any harm comes to her, I will make you suffer for your part in this."

He knew he would never stop searching until he found Lara and could hold her in his arms again.

Epilogue

Even though Thomas suffered, he still had a duty to protect their castle and the humans in the village. Tate had taken on most of the burden, allowing him to continue to search for Lara. Recently, there had been numerous deadly attacks on the village of Echo Bluff and the surrounding villages. The word had spread of attempts to kidnap humans from their homes. Thomas was sure that they were all instigated by Jario. Since moving to Crimson Claw Castle, he had been building a small army of mindless vampires to do his dirty work. Thomas believed that Jario was, somehow, behind the disappearance of Lara. If he was not working with Velsa, he was certain that he had caused her to vanish.

The loss that Thomas felt from Lara's absence was devastating. Six full moons had passed since Lara had vanished, and the pain was still fresh in his mind and body. The time had come to light the lantern in the Evergreen tower. This was done every evening to help guide Lara home. Every evening, he longed for a signal that Lara would come back to him. As Thomas opened the lantern door to light the candle, he felt a flicker of warmth within his chest. It was just a small flicker, and it left as quickly as it came. Rubbing his chest, he thought of the dark night he had lost her. Feeling moisture fill his eyes, he raised his hand to set the candle a glow. The wick of the candle flickered to life on its own. As it did, Thomas felt the warmth return to his chest. This time, it was stronger and filled his entire body. This was the sign he had hoped would come. He knew that Lara was alive! He knew that Lara was alive, and he would be able to find her.

* * *

The spell of six full moons had passed, and Lara slowly opened her eyes to see the moonlight streaming through the bedroom window. She ran her hands over her arms and felt the warmth of her skin beneath them. Happiness filled her thoughts, as she realized the spell had worked. She was really a human. As she put her hands around her slightly swollen belly, she smiled knowing they were finally safe. The witch had hidden the cottage from view while she slept. Now it would be their home. A place for her daughter to grow, play, and learn as a human. She would be safe from the danger of Jario and his threats. It was time to explore her new world, as a human, and prepare for the birth of her daughter.

A NOTE FROM THE AUTHOR

Thank you for reading Escaping Obscurity. I hope you enjoyed reading more about Thomas and Lara. Rest assured, this story does not end with their tragic separation. Thomas' journey to find Lara continues with Protected from Obscurity.

If you enjoyed this book, please take a moment to write a review for Escaping Obscurity on Amazon and Goodreads. Your comments are greatly appreciated.

I would love to hear from readers. You may contact me by email or by leaving a comment on Facebook. I hope to hear from you soon!

info@authorjoannherley.com

https://www.facebook.com/authorjhbooks

Join my mailing list and I will send you an email when my next book is released. Also, anyone that joins my mailing list will receive early notification of giveaways and become eligible for private mailing list giveaways.

www.authorjoannherley.com

OTHER BOOKS BY THE AUTHOR

EVERGREEN SERIES

Book I   Seized by Obscurity

Book II   Escaping Obscurity

Book III Protected from Obscurity (Coming early fall of 2015)

Book IV Shattering Obscurity (Coming early 2016)

www.ingramcontent.com/pod-product-compliance
Lightning Source LLC
Chambersburg PA
CBHW061216170626
46809CB00003B/1378